CLASSIC
FAIRY TALES
TO READ ALOUD

SELECTED BY NAOMI LEWIS

ILLUSTRATED BY JO WORTH

KINGFISHER

Counsel

The face in the water said
(rather fretfully, I thought):
Be courteous to crone and spider,
Prudent with keys,
Free the hooked fish and such –
Of course you know all about that;

And *do* be careful when wishing.
In spite of all the examples
They *never* learn.
It takes imagination
To start with the fourth guess, thought of later,
The fourth wish, after the moral.

NAOMI LEWIS

KINGFISHER
An imprint of Kingfisher Publications Plc
New Penderel House, 283-288 High Holborn
London WC1V 7HZ
www.kingfisherpub.com

First published in hardback by Kingfisher 1996
First published in paperback by Kingfisher 1998
6 8 10 9 7 5
5TR/0603/THOM/HBM(MAR)/100INDWF

A CIP catalogue record for this book
is available from the British Library.

ISBN 0 7534 0287 4

Printed in India

CONTENTS

── INTRODUCTION ──

"The Pot of Soup, the Cauldron of Story, has always been boiling," (Tolkien wrote), "and to it have always been added new bits, dainty and undainty." Helpings from that cauldron are the contents of this book. "But why do you call them fairy tales?" asked a quibbling friend. "Where are the fairies?" They are there, all the way through, whether or not with gauzy wings and tiny wand. In these pages you will find pixies, a goblin, a troll or two, a seal-fairy, a fairy godmother (and daughter), the immortal witch Baba Yaga, and a marvellous unseen spirit ("that which was down the well"). Gifted helpers include a cat, a doll, a wolf, a fish, even a three legged stool. Above all you will find magic itself and its ways to solve all problems.

Still, the question does have an historical answer. The term which we use so easily comes from 17th century France: *conte de fée*. It stood for a tale in which needed supernatural aid came not from the church but an older less rigid power.

Where do they come from, our most familiar stories? A small but essential group (taking in such favourites as "Cinderella", "Puss-in-Boots", "The Sleeping Beauty") we owe to the elegant French of Charles Perrault (1628-1703). Minister, courtier, architect and avoider of anything cruel or vulgar in his tales, he was a kind father to his three young motherless children, probably the first to hear those stories. But the main collecting period was the 19th century. The Grimm brothers, Jacob (1785-1863) and Wilhelm (1786-1859) were the first important gatherers of the rapidly vanishing folk and fairy lore, never yet in print. Their achievement fired Asbjørnsen (1812-85) and Moe (1813-82) in Norway, Afanasiev in Russia and Joseph Jacobs (1854-1916) in England, to compile their own great collections. Stories from all of these are in this book. A curious fact is that the huge Afanasiev volumes were published first in England in the mid 19th century. The crushingly powerful church in Tsarist Russia could not have allowed such secular works the privilege of print.

And Andersen (1805-75), that other great name, what of him? He was no collector, but an inventor, a true original. After a very few tales based on traditional themes, he realised that every thing around him held a story, was a character in its own right. That was something new! His short-lived father, by trade a poor shoemaker but by nature an artist, a rebel thinker, had shown the little Hans Christian how to look at the insects and grasses, how to make small toy theatres. The result is in Andersen's work. His stories, voiced so intimately, just for your personal hearing, are ideal for reading aloud. He was to tell them himself – as in "The Flying Trunk" – to various royal households of that time, an honoured and welcome guest. Remember that until the First World War (1914-18), most of Europe, and Germany in particular, was made up of tiny kingdoms and principalities. No wonder there are so many in fairy tale.

Omissions in this book? Well, no one is more sadly aware of the absent items than the compiler. I'll name just a few that were much too long to include: Andersen's "The Snow Queen", Ruskin's "The King of the Golden River", Wilde's "The Fisherman and his Soul", and Mayne's "A Year and a Day". Space and technical reasons kept out others – the leprechaun tale that I was pursuing seems to have slipped away, in the manner of leprechauns, for instance. But I have tried to give examples of the main classic storylines; sometimes (as in "East O' the Sun and West O' the Moon") one is encased in another story. The notes before each should explain, if briefly, why the tale came to be chosen.

Something more must be said. Repeated myths can have more power than you might think. I have never been easy about the bent and muttering witch, doing horrible things and meeting a no less horrible end. Too often this appalling end is a mirror of actual fact. Not many centuries past (and happening still in parts of the world today), any crazed or deformed or aged woman, living alone in poverty, could be made the target of village hate for some mishap, and be tortured and done to death. The witch tale, mainly imported from Grimm but popular in Britain (our own record in history is none too good) did not help the victims' cause. But the Russian witch Baba Yaga, invincible, a sorceress of quality, with a unique domestic establishment, was a more than worthy foe. No wonder she survives for the next story.

The other wrong, still all too active, concerns the wolf; degraded, shamed and sadistically killed in most of the nursery tales, and in life, by the cruellest means, brought to the edge of extinction. The two, the tale and the fact, are closely related. Yet the wolf, except in defence, is no attacker of man and, indeed, has been known at times to save and bring up abandoned human young. The restored end of "Little Red Riding Hood" (given here) may not be zoologically accurate (would he have eaten the tough old woman?) but it is more honourable than that of the usual altered version. There's an interesting verdict too from a guileless four year old (see the introductory note to the story).

Fairy tales: yes or no? What do you gain by meeting them as a child? Better to start by saying how much is lost if you fail to meet them then, or do so only through cartoon films of the Disney type, or videos. The words are part of the whole. In the landscape of the mind, whatever is planted early lasts and grows through time. Reality may be a featureless urban-suburban street; but the mind of the fairy tale reader holds mountains, oceans, distances, a forest that is haven, shelter and mystery, one day to be explored, with a pathway that leads to the very edge of the world. Adapt this to your liking.

The stories also offer a useful guide to behaviour. Be courteous to crone and spider – or ant, or bird, any creature really. Help given is help returned, at time of greatest need. The baddies never learn that politeness serves you best. Be generous: share your crust. And, above all, wish with care. Think well before you start: your wishes may come true.

In England, not only the rustic people but the serious writers seem to have had an easy acceptance of fairy beings. Descriptions abound in Spenser, Shakespeare, Jonson, Drayton and numerous others; later, even, in 18th century Pope ("The Rape of the Lock"). The engaging antiquarian gossip John Aubrey (1627-97) has a fund of anecdotes about sightings of the little creatures. Here is an instance:

"Not twenty years ago, not far from Cyrencester, there appeared an apparition. Mr Lilly believes it was a fairy, but being demanded whether a good spirit or a bad, it returned no answer, but disappeared with a curious perfume, and a most melodious twang."

Blake (1757-1827) – and who would question *his* visions? – describes a fairy funeral:

"Did you ever see a fairy funeral? I have! I was walking alone in my garden; there was a great stillness in the air; I heard a low and pleasant sound, and I knew not whence it came. At last I saw the broad leaf of a flower move, and underneath it I saw a procession of creatures, of the size and colour of green and grey grasshoppers, bearing a body laid out on a roseleaf, which they buried with songs, and then disappeared. It was a fairy's funeral."

Does all this stand for belief? That's an elusive word. We believe in the moon of song and verse, while we also know that it is huge and cold and grey, pitted with craters. Fairy tales grew out of want and need, hope and dream, desire to defeat the impossible. And in every tale it *is* defeated, a special gift to the listener. What is that gift? Imagination. No wonder Pushkin said, "Each story is a poem." And though today we have light and flight, music and pictures at a touch and all manner of other marvels, are there not other impossibles? So when I am asked now and then if I believe in fairies, as a fairy tale reader I answer with prudence, "Of course. The real question, though, is – do they believe in *me*?"

Naomi Lewis

The Fisherman and his Wife

by

THE BROTHERS GRIMM

based on the translation of

EDGAR TAYLOR

This is one of the great Grimm stories, memorable both for its telling and for what it tells. There is a third point of interest. When the brothers Wilhelm and Jacob began their work of collecting (and rescuing) spoken folk and fairy lore, they were much encouraged by two striking stories, brought to them by a friend who had acquired them (perhaps in rougher form) from an old Pomeranian fisherman. One was "The Fisherman and His Wife". And what does it say? That you can't wish

beyond your own capacity. If you are mean, greedy and envious, if you have never used your imagination on anything but possessions, all the money and luxury in the world won't make you different – or satisfied, or content. Wish carefully: this is a serious rule for all of us, for the wish may come about. What do the big lottery winners do with their terrifying wealth? Are they changed for the better?

As for the telling itself, it has a dramatic pattern that continues to grip the listener. As the poor fisherman timorously brings each time his more and more shaming message, the great fish (who understands him well) speaks few words, shows only an ominous calm. But the increasing wildness and changing colours of sea and sky powerfully reflect the truth.

There was once a fisherman who lived with his wife in a hovel, close to the sea. The fisherman used to go out all day a-fishing; and one day, as he sat on the shore with his rod, looking at the shining water and watching his line, all of a sudden his float was dragged away deep under the sea: and in drawing it up he pulled a great fish, a flounder, out of the water. The fish said to him, "Pray let me live. I am not a real fish, I am an enchanted prince. Put me in the water again, and let me go." "Oh!" said the man, "you need not make so many words about the matter. I wish to have nothing to do with a fish that can talk, so swim away as soon as you please." Then he put him back into the water, and the fish darted straight down to the bottom, and left a long streak of blood behind him.

When the fisherman went home to his wife in the hovel, he told her how he had caught a great fish, and how it had told him it was an enchanted prince, and that on hearing it speak he had let it go again. "Did you not ask it for anything?" said the wife. "No," said the man, "what should I ask for?" "Ah!" said the wife, "we live very wretchedly here in this nasty stinking hovel; do go back, and tell the fish we want a little cottage."

The fisherman did not much like the business: however, he went to the sea, and when he came there the water looked all yellow and green. And he stood at the water's edge, and said,

> *"Flounder, flounder in the sea,*
> *I prithee hearken unto me.*
> *Ilse, my wife, will have her way*
> *Whatever I do, whatever I say."*

Then the fish came swimming to him, and said, "Well, what does she want?" "Ah!" answered the fisherman, "my wife says that when I had caught you, I ought to have asked you for something before I let you go again. She says she won't live a minute longer in the hovel. She wants a little cottage." "Go home, then," said the fish, "she is in the cottage already." So the man went home, and saw his wife standing at the door of a cottage. "Come in, come in," said she; "is not this much better than the ditch?" And there was a parlour, and a bed-chamber, and a kitchen; and behind the cottage there was a little garden with all sorts of flowers and fruits, and a courtyard full of ducks and chickens. "Ah!" said the fisherman, "how happily we shall live!" "We will try to do so at least," said his wife.

Everything went right for a week or two, and then the wife said, "Husband, there is not room enough in this cottage, the courtyard and garden are a great deal too small. I should like to have a large stone castle to live in, so go to the fish again, and tell him to give us a castle." "Wife," said the fisherman, "I don't like to go to him again, for perhaps he will be angry; we ought to be content with the cottage." "Nonsense!" said the wife. "He will do it very willingly; go along, and try."

The fisherman went; but his heart was very heavy: and when he came to the sea, it looked blue and gloomy, though it was quite calm, and he went close to it, and said,

> "Flounder, flounder in the sea,
> I prithee hearken unto me.
> Ilse, my wife, will have her way
> Whatever I do, whatever I say."

"Well, what does she want now?" said the fish. "Ah!" said the man very sorrowfully, "my wife wants to live in a stone castle." "Go home then," said the fish, "she is standing at the door of it already." So away went the fisherman, and found his wife standing before a great castle. "See," said she, "is not this grand?" With that they went into the castle together, and found a great many servants there, and the rooms all richly furnished and full of golden chairs and tables; and behind the castle was a garden, and a wood half a mile long, full of sheep, and goats, and hares, and deer; and in the courtyard were stables and cowhouses. "Well," said the man, "now will we live contented and happy in this beautiful castle for the rest of our lives." "Perhaps we may," said the wife; "but let us consider and sleep upon it before we make up our minds." So they went to bed.

The next morning, when the wife awoke, it was broad daylight, and she jogged the fisherman with her elbow, and said, "Get up, husband, and bestir yourself, for we must be king of all the land." "Wife, wife," said the man, "why should we wish to be king? I will not be king." "Then I will," said the wife. "But, wife," answered the fisherman, "how can you be king? The fish cannot make you a king." "Husband," said she, "say no more about it, but go and try; I will be king!" So the man went away, quite sorrowful to think that his wife should want to be king. The sea looked a dark grey colour, and was covered with foam as he cried out,

> *"Flounder, flounder in the sea,*
> *I prithee hearken unto me.*
> *Ilse, my wife, will have her way*
> *Whatever I do, whatever I say."*

"Well, what would she have now?" said the fish. "Alas!" said the man, "my wife wants to be king." "Go home," said the fish; "she is king already."

Then the fisherman went home; and as he came close to the palace, he saw a troop of soldiers, and heard the sound of drums and trumpets; and when he entered in, he saw his wife sitting on a high throne of gold and diamonds, with a golden crown upon her head; and on each side of her stood six beautiful maidens, each a head taller than the other. "Well, wife," said the fisherman, "are you king?" "Yes," said she, "I am king." And when he had looked at her for a long time, he said, "Ah, wife! what a fine thing it is to be king! Now we shall never have anything more to wish for."

"I don't know how that may be," said she, "never is a long time. I am king, 'tis true, but I begin to be tired of it, and I think I should like to be emperor." "Alas, wife! Why should you wish to be emperor?" said the fisherman. "Husband," said she, "go to the fish; I say I will be emperor." "Ah, wife!" replied the fisherman. "The fish cannot make an emperor, and I should not like to ask for such a thing." "I am king," said the wife, "and you are my slave, so go directly!" So the fisherman was obliged to go; and he muttered as he went along. "This will come to no good, it is too much to ask, the fish will be tired at last, and then we shall repent of what we have done." He soon arrived at the sea, and the water was quite black and muddy, and a mighty whirlwind blew over it; but he went to the shore, and said,

> *"Flounder, flounder in the sea,*
> *I prithee hearken unto me.*
> *Ilse, my wife, will have her way*
> *Whatever I do, whatever I say."*

"What would she have now?" said the fish. "Ah!" said the fisherman. "She wants to be emperor." "Go home," said the fish, "she is emperor already."

So he went home again; and as he came near he saw his wife sitting on a very lofty throne made of solid gold, with a great crown on her head full two yards high, and on each side of her stood her guards and attendants in a row, each one smaller than the other, from the tallest giant down to a little dwarf no bigger than my finger. And before her stood princes, and dukes, and earls: and the fisherman went up to her and said, "Wife, are you emperor?" "Yes," said she, "I am emperor." "Ah!" said the man as he gazed upon her, "what a fine thing it is to be emperor!" "Husband," said she, "why should we stay at being emperor; I will be pope next." "O wife, wife!" said he. "How can you be pope? There is but one pope at a time in Christendom." "Husband," said she, "I will be pope this very day." "But," replied the husband, "the fish cannot make you pope." "What nonsense!" said she. "If he can make an emperor, he can make a pope, go and try him." So the fisherman went. But when he came to the shore the wind was raging, and the sea was tossed up and down like boiling water, and the ships were in the greatest distress and danced upon the waves most fearfully; in the middle of the sky there was a little blue, but towards the south it was all red as if a dreadful storm was rising. At this the fisherman was terribly frightened, and trembled, so that his knees knocked together: but he went to the shore and said,

> *"Flounder, flounder in the sea,*
> *I prithee hearken unto me.*
> *Ilse, my wife, will have her way*
> *Whatever I do, whatever I say."*

"What does she want now?" said the fish. "Ah!" said the fisherman. "My wife wants to be pope." "Go home," said the fish, "she is pope already."

Then the fisherman went home, and found his wife sitting on a throne that was two miles high; and she had three great crowns on her head, and around stood all the pomp and power of the Church; and on each side were two rows of burning lights, of all sizes, the greatest as large as the highest and biggest tower in the world, and the least no larger than a small rushlight. "Wife," said the fisherman as he looked at all this grandeur, "are you pope?" "Yes," said she, "I am pope." "Well, wife," replied he, "it is a grand thing to be pope; and now you must be content, for you can be nothing greater." "I will consider of that," said the wife. Then they went to bed: but the wife could not sleep all night for thinking what she should be next. At last morning came, and the sun rose. "Ha!" thought she as she looked at it through the window. "Cannot I prevent the sun rising?" At this she was very angry, and she wakened her husband, and said, "Husband, go to the fish and tell him I want to be lord of the sun and moon." The fisherman was half asleep, but the thought frightened him so much, that he started and fell out of bed. "Alas, wife!" said he. "Cannot you be content to be pope?" "No," said she, "I am very uneasy, and cannot bear to see the sun and moon rise without my leave. Go to the fish directly."

Then the man went trembling for fear; and as he was going down to the shore a dreadful storm arose, so that the trees and the rocks shook; and the heavens became black, and the lightning played, and the thunder rolled; and you might have seen in the sea great black waves like mountains with a white crown of foam upon them; and the fisherman said,

"Flounder, flounder in the sea,
I prithee hearken unto me.
Ilse, my wife, will have her way
Whatever I do, whatever I say."

"What does she want now?" said the fish. "Ah!" said he, "she wants to be lord of the sun and moon." "Go home," said the fish, "to your hovel again!" And there they live to this very day.

LITTLE RED RIDING HOOD

by

CHARLES PERRAULT

translated by

ANGELA CARTER

One of the best known of all "nursery" tales, this comes to us from Perrault (see the Introduction). His three young motherless children must have heard it often from their father or their nurse. Why is it so familiar? The answer, I suspect, is in the title. Without the red hood and cloak, which give the girl a name as well, would she have stayed in our minds? But later centuries have made changes to the ending. In Perrault's telling, the wolf does not have his usual unpleasant fate: he

*comes out the winner! He is, you could say, the worker of the moral.
And Perrault's moral (to be summed up briefly as young girls, beware
of smooth-tongued strangers, posing as kindly wolves) is as timely now
as ever it was. You can scarcely ever find the original version today –
but you have it here. Lang, who uses the original in his* Blue Fairy Book
*(1897), called the modern changes "a perversion of history. Probably,"
he adds, "children prefer the truth." What's your opinion?*

*Lang also tells a charming tale of a four-year-old little girl in
Perrault's time, who listened to the tale with close attention. At the end,
she cried out: "O, le gentil petit loup!" ("The kind little wolf!"). Her
interest was in the cake or custard tart in the basket. The wolf may have
gobbled up some humans, but he had kindly left the cake.*

Once upon a time, deep in the heart of the country,
there lived a pretty little girl whose mother adored
her, and her grandmother adored her even more. This
good woman made her a red hood like the ones that fine
ladies wear when they go riding. The hood suited the child so
much that soon everybody was calling her Little Red Riding
Hood.

One day, her mother baked some cakes on the griddle and
said to Little Red Riding Hood:

"Your granny is sick; you must go and visit her. Take her
one of these cakes and a little pot of butter."

Little Red Riding Hood went off to the next village to visit
her grandmother. As she walked through the wood, she met a
wolf, who wanted to eat her but did not dare to because there
were woodcutters working nearby. He asked her where she
was going. The poor child did not know how dangerous it is

to chatter away to wolves and replied innocently:

"I'm going to visit my grandmother to take her this cake and this little pot of butter from my mother."

"Does your grandmother live far away?" asked the wolf.

"Oh yes," said Little Red Riding Hood. "She lives beyond the mill you can see over there, in the first house you come to in the village."

"Well, I shall go and visit her, too," said the wolf. "I will take *this* road and you shall take *that* road and let's see who can get there first."

The wolf ran off by the shortest path and Red Riding Hood went off the longest way and she made it still longer because she dawdled along, gathering nuts and chasing butterflies and picking bunches of wayside flowers.

The wolf soon arrived at Grandmother's house. He knocked on the door, rat tat tat.

"Who's there?"

"Your grand-daughter, Little Red Riding Hood," said the wolf, disguising his voice. "I've brought you a cake baked on the griddle and a little pot of butter from my mother."

Grandmother was lying in bed because she was poorly. She called out:

"Lift up the latch and walk in!"

The wolf lifted the latch and opened the door. He had not eaten for three days. He threw himself on the good woman and gobbled her up. Then he closed the door behind him and lay down in Grandmother's bed to wait for Little Red Riding Hood. At last she came knocking on the door, rat tat tat.

"Who's there?"

Little Red Riding Hood heard the hoarse voice of the wolf and thought that her grandmother must have caught a cold. She answered:

"It's your grand-daughter, Little Red Riding Hood. I've brought you a cake baked on the griddle and a little pot of butter from my mother."

The wolf disguised his voice and said:

"Lift up the latch and walk in."

Little Red Riding Hood lifted the latch and opened the door.

When the wolf saw her come in, he hid himself under the bedclothes and said to her:

"Put the cake and the butter down on the bread-bin and come and lie down with me."

Little Red Riding Hood took off her clothes and went to lie down in the bed. She was surprised to see how odd her grandmother looked. She said to her:

"Grandmother, what big arms you have!"

"All the better to hold you with, my dear."

"Grandmother, what big legs you have!"

"All the better to run with, my dear."

"Grandmother, what big ears you have!"

"All the better to hear with, my dear."

"Grandmother, what big eyes you have!"

"All the better to see with, my dear!"

"Grandmother, what big teeth you have!"

"All the better to eat you up!"

At that, the wicked wolf threw himself upon Little Red Riding Hood and gobbled her up, too.

MORAL

Children, especially pretty, nicely brought-up young ladies, ought never to talk to strangers; if they are foolish enough to do so, they should not be surprised if some greedy wolf consumes them, elegant red riding hoods and all.

Now, there are real wolves, with hairy pelts and enormous teeth; but also wolves who seem perfectly charming, sweet-natured and obliging, who pursue young girls in the street and pay them the most flattering attentions.

Unfortunately, these smooth-tongued, smooth-pelted wolves are the most dangerous beasts of all.

EAST O' THE SUN AND WEST O' THE MOON

by

ASBJØRNSEN & MOE

translated by

SIR GEORGE DASENT

If a single story had to be chosen to represent traditional Western fairy tale at its best and most magical (and that includes the telling) it might be hard to find a likelier candidate than this. (The title itself is a bonus.)

It comes from that mine of story, the classic Norwegian collection of 1844 (Norske Folkeeventyr) made by P.C. Asbjørnsen and J. Moe. As young enthusiasts they had been fired by the Grimms' example. The first (and arguably still the best) translation into English was Sir George Dasent's Popular Tales from the Norse *(1859). Dasent was a crotchety character but a matchless storyteller; you can just catch his engaging Scottish voice in the pages here. ("'Maybe you are the lassie that ought to have had him?' Yes, she was.")*

But what especially marks the tale is the number of themes and features that run together so naturally through its course. There is scarcely room to do more than list them: the animal-human husband, one not to be seen in human form; the doing of the forbidden thing; the quest; the spell to be broken; wise old crones who know it all, past and future; towering cliffs and crags; castles dangerous – and more. The White Bear's brisk arrival seems to foreshadow the Beauty-and-Beast situation; in a way it does, but differently. The bear in the tale is no monster; in the North he was even held to be King of the beasts. The great ride with the North Wind, "so wild and cross, 'twas gruesome to look at him", belongs with the many memorable rides of story: don't forget that speed over distances, let alone aerial flight, was impossible, whether to king or peasant. Well, if you need to get to the end of the world, the answer is in the tale. "Thither you'll come, late or never." And you will.

O nce on a time there was a poor husbandman who had so many children that he hadn't much of either food or clothing to give them. Pretty children they all were, but the prettiest was the youngest daughter, who was so lovely there was no end to her loveliness.

So one day, 'twas on a Thursday evening late at the fall of the year, the weather was so wild and rough outside, and it was so cruelly dark, and rain fell and wind blew, till the walls of the cottage shook again. There they all sat round the fire busy with this thing and that. But just then, all at once something gave three taps on the windowpane. Then the father went out to see what was the matter; and, when he got out of doors, what should he see but a great big White Bear.

"Good evening to you," said the White Bear.

"The same to you," said the man.

"Will you give me your youngest daughter? If you will, I'll make you as rich as you are now poor," said the Bear.

Well, the man would not be at all sorry to be so rich; but still he thought he must have a bit of a talk with his daughter first; so he went in and told them how there was a great White Bear waiting outside, who had given his word to make them so rich if he could only have the youngest daughter.

The lassie said "No!" outright. Nothing could get her to say anything else; so the man went out and settled it with the White Bear, that he should come again the next Thursday evening and get an answer. Meantime he talked his daughter over, and kept on telling her of all the riches they would get, and how well off she would be herself; and so at last she thought better of it, and washed and mended her rags, made herself as smart as she could, and was ready to start. I can't say her packing gave her much trouble.

Next Thursday evening came the White Bear to fetch her, and she got upon his back with her bundle, and off they went. So, when they had gone a bit of the way, the White Bear said—

"Are you afraid?"

"No!" she wasn't.

"Well! mind and hold tight by my shaggy coat, and then there's nothing to fear," said the Bear.

So she rode a long, long way, till they came to a great steep hill. There, on the face of it, the White Bear gave a knock, and a door opened, and they came into a castle, where there were many rooms all lit up; rooms gleaming with silver and gold; and there too was a table ready laid, and it was all as grand as grand could be. Then the White Bear gave her a silver bell; and when she wanted anything, she was only to ring it, and she would get it at once.

Well, after she had eaten and drunk, and evening wore on, she got sleepy after her journey, and thought she would like to go to bed, so she rang the bell; and she had scarce taken hold of it before she came into a chamber, where there was a bed made, as fair and white as anyone would wish to sleep in, with silken pillows and curtains, and gold fringe. All that was in the room was gold or silver; but when she had gone to bed, and put out the light, a man came and laid himself alongside her. That was the White Bear, who threw off his beast shape at night; but she never saw him, for he always came after she had put out the light, and before the day dawned he was up and off again. So things went on happily for a while but at last she began to get silent and sorrowful; for there she went about all day alone, and she longed to go home to see her father and mother, and brothers and sisters. So one day, when the White Bear asked what it was that she lacked, she said it was so dull and lonely there, and how she longed to go home to see her father and mother, and brothers and sisters, and that was why she was so sad and sorrowful, because she couldn't get to them.

"Well, well!" said the Bear, "perhaps there's a cure for all this; but you must promise me one thing, not to talk alone with your mother, but only when the rest are by to hear; for she'll take you by the hand and try to lead you into a room alone to talk; but you must mind and not do that, else you'll bring bad luck on both of us."

So one Sunday the White Bear came and said now they could set off to see her father and mother. Well, off they started, she sitting on his back; and they went far and long. At last they came to a grand house, and there her brothers and sisters were running about out of doors at play, and everything was so pretty, 'twas a joy to see.

"This is where your father and mother live now," said the White Bear; "but don't forget what I told you, else you'll make us both unlucky."

"No! bless her, she'd not forget"; and when she had reached the house, the White Bear turned right about and left her.

Then when she went in to see her father and mother, there was such joy, there was no end to it. None of them thought they could thank her enough for all she had done for them. Now, they had everything they wished, as good as good could be, and they all wanted to know how she got on where she lived.

Well, she said, it was very good to live where she did; she

had all she wished. What she said beside I don't know; but I don't think any of them had the right end of the stick, or that they got much out of her. But so in the afternoon, after they had done dinner, all happened as the White Bear had said. Her mother wanted to talk with her alone in her bedroom; but she minded what the White Bear had said, and wouldn't go upstairs.

"Oh, what we have to talk about will keep," she said, and put her mother off. But somehow or other, her mother got round her at last, and she had to tell her the whole story. So she said, how every night, when she had gone to bed, a man came and lay down beside her as soon as she had put out the light, and how she never saw him, because he was always up and away before the morning dawned; and how she went about woeful and sorrowing, for she thought she should so like to see him, and how all day long she walked about there alone, and how dull, and dreary, and lonesome it was.

"My!" said her mother; "it may well be a Troll you slept with! But now I'll teach you a lesson how to set eyes on him. I'll give you a bit of candle, which you can carry home in your bosom; just light that while he is asleep, but take care not to drop the tallow on him."

Yes! she took the candle, and hid it in her bosom, and as night drew on, the White Bear came and fetched her away.

But when they had gone a bit of the way, the White Bear asked if all hadn't happened as he had said.

"Well, she couldn't say it hadn't."

"Now, mind," said he, "if you have listened to your

mother's advice, you have brought bad luck on us both, and then, all that has passed between us will be as nothing."

"No," she said, "she hadn't listened to her mother's advice."

So when she reached home, and had gone to bed, it was the old story over again. There came a man and lay down beside her; but at dead of night, when she heard he slept, she got up and struck a light, lit the candle, and let the light shine on him, and so she saw that he was the loveliest Prince one ever set eyes on, and she fell so deeply in love with him on the spot, that she thought she couldn't live if she didn't give him a kiss there and then. And so she did, but as she kissed him, she dropped three hot drops of tallow on his shirt, and he woke up.

"What have you done?" he cried; "now you have made us both unlucky, for had you held out only this one year, I had been freed. For I have a stepmother who has bewitched me, so that I am a White Bear by day, and a Man by night. But now all ties are snapped between us; now I must set off from you to her. She lives in a castle which stands EAST O' THE SUN AND WEST O' THE MOON, and there, too, is a Princess, with a nose three ells long, and she's the wife I must have now."

She wept and took it ill, but there was no help for it; go he must.

Then she asked if she mightn't go with him.

No, she mightn't.

"Tell me the way, then," she said, "and I'll search you out; that surely I may get leave to do."

"Yes, she might do that," he said; "but there was no way to that place. It lay EAST O' THE SUN AND WEST O' THE MOON, and thither she'd never find her way."

So next morning, when she woke up, both Prince and castle were gone, and then she lay on a little green patch, in the midst of the gloomy thick wood, and by her side lay the same bundle of rags she had brought with her from her old home.

So when she had rubbed the sleep out of her eyes, and wept till she was tired, she set out on her way, and walked many, many days, till she came to a lofty crag. Under it sat an old hag, and played with a gold apple which she tossed about. Her the lassie asked if she knew the way to the Prince, who lived with his stepmother in the castle that lay EAST O' THE SUN AND WEST O' THE MOON, and who was to marry the Princess with a nose three ells long.

"How did you come to know about him?" asked the old hag; "but maybe you are the lassie who ought to have had him?"

Yes, she was.

"So, so; it's you, is it?" said the old hag. "Well, all I know about him is, that he lives in the castle that lies EAST O' THE SUN AND WEST O' THE MOON, and thither you'll come, late or never; but still you may have the loan of my horse, and on him you can ride to my next neighbour. Maybe she'll be able to tell you; and when you get there, just give the horse a switch under the left ear, and beg him to be off home; and, stay, this gold apple you may take with you."

So she got upon the horse, and rode a long, long time, till

she came to another crag, under which sat another old hag, with a gold carding comb. Her the lassie asked if she knew the way to the castle that lay EAST O' THE SUN AND WEST O' THE MOON, and she answered, like the first old hag, that she knew nothing about it, except it was east of the sun and west of the moon.

"And thither you'll come, late or never; but you shall have the loan of my horse to my next neighbour; maybe she'll tell you all about it; and when you get there, just switch the horse under the left ear, and beg him to be off home."

And this old hag gave her the golden carding comb; it might be she'd find some use for it, she said. So the lassie got up on the horse, and rode a far far way, and a weary time; and so at last she came to another great crag, under which sat another old hag, spinning with a golden spinning wheel. Her, too, she asked if she knew the way to the Prince, and where the castle was that lay EAST O' THE SUN AND WEST O' THE MOON. So it was the same thing over again.

"Maybe it's you who ought to have had the Prince?" said the old hag.

Yes, it was.

But she, too, didn't know the way a bit better than the other two. "East o' the sun and west o' the moon it was," she knew – that was all.

"And thither you'll come, late or never; but I'll lend you my horse, and then I think you'd best ride to the East Wind and ask him; maybe he knows those parts, and can blow you thither. But when you get to him, you need only give the horse a switch under the left ear, and he'll trot home of himself."

And so, too, she gave her the gold spinning wheel. "Maybe you'll find a use for it," said the old hag.

Then on she rode many many days, a weary time, before she got to the East Wind's house, but at last she did reach it, and then she asked the East Wind if he could tell her the way to the Prince who dwelt east of the sun and west of the moon. Yes, the East Wind had often heard tell of it, the Prince and the castle, but he couldn't tell the way, for he had never blown so far.

"But, if you will, I'll go with you to my brother the West Wind, maybe he knows, for he's much stronger. So, if you will just get on my back, I'll carry you thither."

Yes, she got on his back, and I should just think they went briskly along.

So when they got there, they went into the West Wind's house, and the East Wind said the lassie he had brought was the one who ought to have had the Prince who lived in the castle EAST O' THE SUN AND WEST O' THE MOON; and so she had set out to seek him, and how he had come with her, and would be glad to know if the West Wind knew how to get to the castle.

"Nay," said the West Wind, "so far I've never blown; but if you will, I'll go with you to our brother the South Wind, for he's much stronger than either of us, and he has flapped his wings far and wide. Maybe he'll tell you. You can get on my back, and I'll carry you to him."

Yes! she got on his back, and so they travelled to the South

Wind, and weren't so very long on the way, I should think.

When they got there, the West Wind asked him if he could tell her the way to the castle that lay EAST O' THE SUN AND WEST O' THE MOON, for it was she who ought to have had the Prince who lived there.

"You don't say so! That's she, is it?" said the South Wind.

"Well, I have blustered about in most places in my time, but so far have I never blown; but if you will, I'll take you to my brother the North Wind; he is the oldest and strongest of the whole lot of us, and if he don't know where it is, you'll never find anyone in the world to tell you. You can get on my back, and I'll carry you thither."

Yes! she got on his back, and away he went from his house at a fine rate. And this time, too, she wasn't long on her way.

So when they got to the North Wind's house, he was so wild and cross, cold puffs came from him a long way off.

"BLAST YOU BOTH, WHAT DO YOU WANT?" he roared out to them ever so far off, so that it struck them with an icy shiver.

"Well," said the South Wind, "you needn't be so foul-mouthed, for here I am, your brother, the South Wind, and here is the lassie who ought to have had the Prince who dwells in the castle that lies EAST O' THE SUN AND WEST O' THE MOON, and now she wants to ask you if you ever were there, and can tell her the way, for she would be so glad to find him again."

"YES, I KNOW WELL ENOUGH WHERE IT IS," said the North Wind; "once in my life I blew an aspen leaf thither, but I was so tired I couldn't blow a puff for ever so many days after. But if you really wish to go thither, and aren't afraid to come along with me, I'll take you on my back and see if I can blow you thither."

Yes! with all her heart; she must and would get thither if it were possible in any way; and as for fear, however madly he went, she wouldn't be at all afraid.

"Very well, then," said the North Wind, "but you must sleep here tonight, for we must have the whole day before us, if we're to get thither at all."

Early next morning the North Wind woke her, and puffed himself up, and blew himself out, and made himself so stout and big, 'twas gruesome to look at him; and so off they went high up through the air, as if they would never stop till they got to the world's end.

Down here below there was such a storm; it threw down long tracts of wood and many houses, and when it swept over the great sea, ships foundered by hundreds.

So they tore on and on – no one can believe how far they went – and all the while they still went over the sea, and the North Wind got more and more weary, and so out of breath he could scarce bring out a puff, and his wings drooped and drooped, till at last he sunk so low that the crests of the waves dashed over his heels.

"Are you afraid?" said the North Wind.

"No!" she wasn't.

But they weren't very far from land; and the North Wind had still so much strength left in him that he managed to throw her up on the shore under the windows of the castle which lay EAST O' THE SUN AND WEST O' THE MOON; but then he was so weak and worn out, he had to stay there and rest many days before he could get home again.

Next morning the lassie sat down under the castle window, and began to play with the gold apple; and the first person she saw was the Long-nose who was to have the Prince.

"What do you want for your gold apple, you lassie?" said the Long-nose, and threw up the window.

"It's not for sale, for gold or money," said the lassie.

"If it's not for sale for gold or money, what is it that you will sell it for? You may name your own price," said the Princess.

"Well! if I may get to the Prince, who lives here, and be with him tonight, you shall have it," said the lassie whom the North Wind had brought.

Yes! she might; that could be done. So the Princess got the gold apple; but when the lassie came up to the Prince's bedroom at night he was fast asleep; she called him and shook him, and between whiles she wept sore; but all she could do she couldn't wake him up. Next morning as soon as day broke, came the Princess with the long nose, and drove her out again.

So in the daytime she sat down under the castle windows and began to card with her golden carding comb, and the same thing happened. The Princess asked what she wanted for it; and she said it wasn't for sale for gold or money, but if she might get leave to go up to the Prince and be with him that night, the Princess should have it. But when she went up she found him fast asleep again, and all she called, and all she shook, and wept, and prayed, she couldn't get life into him; and as soon as the first grey peep of day came, then came the Princess with the long nose, and chased her out again.

So in the daytime the lassie sat down outside under the castle window, and began to spin with her golden spinning wheel, and that, too, the Princess with the long nose wanted to have. So she threw up the window and asked what she wanted for it. The lassie said, as she had said twice before, it wasn't for sale for gold or money; but if she might go up to the Prince who was there, and be with him alone that night, she might have it.

Yes! she might do that and welcome. But now you must know there were some Christian folk who had been carried off thither, and as they sat in their room, which was next the Prince, they had heard how a woman had been in there, and wept and prayed, and called to him two nights running, and they told that to the Prince.

That evening, when the Princess came with her sleepy drink, the Prince made as if he drank, but threw it over his shoulder, for he could guess it was a sleepy drink. So, when the lassie came in, she found the Prince wide awake; and then she told him the whole story how she had come thither.

"Ah," said the Prince, "you've just come in the very nick of time, for tomorrow is to be our wedding day; but now I won't have the Long-nose, and you are the only woman in the world who can set me free. I'll say I want to see what my wife is fit for, and beg her to wash the shirt which has the three spots of tallow on it; she'll say yes, for she doesn't know 'tis you who put them there; but that's a work only for Christian folk, and not for such a pack of Trolls, and so I'll say that I won't have any other for my bride than the woman who can wash them out, and ask you to do it."

So there was great joy and love between them all that night. But next day, when the wedding was to be, the Prince said—

"First of all, I'd like to see what my bride is fit for."

"Yes!" said the stepmother, with all her heart.

"Well," said the Prince, "I've got a fine shirt which I'd like for my wedding shirt, but somehow or other it has got three spots of tallow on it, which I must have washed out; and I have sworn never to take any other bride than the woman who's able to do that. If she can't, she's not worth having."

Well, that was no great thing they said, so they agreed, and she with the long nose began to wash away as hard as she could, but the more she rubbed and scrubbed, the bigger the spots grew.

"Ah!" said the old hag, her mother, "you can't wash; let me try."

But she hadn't long taken the shirt in hand, before it got far worse than ever, and with all her rubbing, and wringing, and scrubbing, the spots grew bigger and blacker, and the darker and uglier was the shirt.

Then all the other Trolls began to wash, but the longer it lasted, the blacker and uglier the shirt grew, till at last it was as black all over as if it had been up the chimney.

"Ah!" said the Prince, "you're none of you worth a straw:

you can't wash. Why there, outside, sits a beggar lassie, I'll be bound she knows how to wash better than the whole lot of you. COME IN, LASSIE!" he shouted.

Well, in she came.

"Can you wash this shirt clean, lassie, you?" said he.

"I don't know," she said, "but I think I can."

And almost before she had taken it and dipped it in the water, it was as white as driven snow, and whiter still.

"Yes; you are the lassie for me," said the Prince.

At that the old hag flew into such a rage, she burst on the spot, and the Princess with the long nose after her, and the whole pack of Trolls after her – at least I've never heard a word about them since.

As for the Prince and Princess, they set free all the poor Christian folk who had been carried off and shut up there; and they took with them all the silver and gold, and flitted away as far as they could from the castle that lay EAST O' THE SUN AND WEST O' THE MOON.

THE WOMAN OF THE SEA

by

HELEN WADDELL

The fairy creature of this tale is of a rare kind, geographically speaking. The silkie, a seal in the sea, a human on land, with its centuries of legend, song, belief, belongs almost entirely to the Hebrides and the furthest islands of the Scottish north, most richly in the Orkneys and the Shetlands. "Almost" suggests an exception; that exception is a part of Norway's western coast.

What do these beliefs and legends tell? When seals take human shape (we learn), they are more beautiful than any earthbound mortal. They mate with earthly humans (what other theme could there be for tales and ballads?) but, to the human, the union will bring sorrow. For the silkie never loses its desire to return to the sea. However, (as no doubt with the islanders themselves) male and female silkies differ in temperament. The silkie maiden, a gentle creature, is usually taken against her will by the stealing of her seal skin – as in the story here. The silkie male, by contrast (with maybe, one folklorist offers, a hint of Viking ancestry) is the pursuer. For the best of all accounts of such a seal-and-human union you must read that riveting ballad "The Grey Selchie of Sule Skerry". (It is in the Oxford Book of Ballads, *and elsewhere.) The setting is Norway ("In Norway there lived a maid") but the poem was found in the Orkneys, in Orkney dialect. A stranger speaks to this maiden on the shore. She asks the man who he is, where he dwells.*

"I am a man upon the land,
I am a selchie in the sea.
And when I'm far from any strand
My dwelling is in Sule Skerry."

For a while they live together on land. But she refuses to marry the silkie, and he takes their seven year old boy with him down into the sea. As he leaves, he tells her that she will marry "a gunner good", who will shoot dead her silkie son. And so it befalls. Helen Waddell (1889-1965), a fine writer, at once fey and scholarly, was a legend herself in her younger days with her works – much to the taste of the time – on medieval lyrics, saints and such. She fittingly tells the story here.

One clear summer night, a young man was walking on the sand by the sea on the Isle of Unst. He had been all day in the hayfields and was come down to the shore to cool himself, for it was the full moon and the wind blowing fresh off the water.

As he came to the shore he saw the sand shining white in the moonlight and on it the sea-people dancing. He had never seen them before, for they show themselves like seals by day, but on this night, because it was midsummer and a full moon, they were dancing for joy. Here and there he saw dark patches where they had flung down their sealskins, but they themselves were as clear as the moon itself, and they cast no shadow.

He crept a little nearer, and his own shadow moved before him, and of a sudden one of the sea-people danced upon it. The dance was broken. They looked about and saw him and with a cry they fled to their sealskins and dived into the waves. The air was full of their soft crying and splashing.

But one of the fairy people ran hither and thither on the sands, wringing her hands as if she had lost something. The young man looked and saw a patch of darkness in his own shadow. It was a seal's skin. Quickly he threw it behind a rock and watched to see what the sea-fairy would do.

She ran down to the edge of the sea and stood with her feet in the foam, crying to her people to wait for her, but they had gone too far to hear. The moon shone on her and the young man thought she was the loveliest creature he had ever seen. Then she began to weep softly to herself and the sound of it was so pitiful that he could bear it no longer. He stood upright and went down to her.

"What have you lost, woman of the sea?" he asked her.

She turned at the sound of his voice and looked at him, terrified. For a moment he thought she was going to dive into the sea. Then she came a step nearer and held up her two hands to him.

"Sir," she said, "give it back to me and I and my people will give you the treasure of the sea." Her voice was like the waves singing in a shell.

"I would rather have you than the treasure of the sea," said the young man. Although she hid her face in her hands and fell again to crying, more hopeless than ever, he was not moved.

"It is my wife you shall be," he said. "Come with me now to the priest, and we will go home to our own house, and it is yourself shall be mistress of all I have. It is warm you will be in the long winter nights, sitting at your own hearth stone and the peat burning red, instead of swimming in the cold green sea."

She tried to tell him of the bottom of the sea where there comes neither snow nor darkness of night and the waves are as warm as a river in summer, but he would not listen. Then he threw his cloak around her and lifted her in his arms and they were married in the priest's house.

He brought her home to his little thatched cottage and into the kitchen with its earthen floor, and set her down before the hearth in the red glow of the peat. She cried out when she saw the fire, for she thought it was a strange crimson jewel.

"Have you anything as bonny as that in the sea?" he asked her, kneeling down beside her and she said, so faintly that he could scarcely hear her, "No."

"I know not what there is in the sea," he said, "but there is nothing on land as bonny as you." For the first time she ceased her crying and sat looking into the heart of the fire. It was the first thing that made her forget, even for a moment, the sea which was her home.

All the days she was in the young man's house, she never lost the wonder of the fire and it was the first thing she brought her children to see. For she had three children in the twice seven years she lived with him. She was a good wife to him. She baked his bread and she spun the wool from the fleece of his Shetland sheep.

He never named the seal's skin to her, nor she to him, and he thought she was content, for he loved her dearly and she was happy with her children. Once, when he was ploughing on the headland above the bay, he looked down and saw her standing on the rocks and crying in a mournful voice to a great seal in the water. He said nothing when he came home, for he thought to himself it was not to wonder at if she were lonely for the sight of her own people. As for the seal's skin, he had hidden it well.

There came a September evening and she was busy in the house, and the children playing hide-and-seek in the stacks in the gloaming. She heard them shouting and went out to them.

"What have you found?" she said.

The children came running to her. "It is like a big cat," they said, "but it is softer than a cat. Look!" She looked and saw her seal's skin that was hidden under last year's hay.

She gazed at it, and for a long time she stood still. It was warm dusk and the air was yellow with the afterglow of the sunset. The children had run away again, and their voices among the stacks sounded like the voices of birds. The hens were on the roost already and now and then one of them clucked in its sleep. The air was full of little friendly noises from the sleepy talking of the swallows under the thatch. The door was open and the warm smell of the baking of bread came out to her.

She turned to go in, but a small breath of wind rustled over the stacks and she stopped again. It brought a sound that she had heard so long she never seemed to hear it at all. It was the sea whispering down on the sand. Far out on the rocks the great waves broke in a boom, and close in on the sand the little waves slipped racing back. She took up the seal's skin and went swiftly down the track that led to the sands. The children saw her and cried to her to wait for them, but she did not hear them. She was just out of sight when their father came in from the byre and they ran to tell him.

"Which road did she take?" said he.

"The low road to the sea," they answered, but already their father was running to the shore. The children tried to follow him, but their voices died away behind him, so fast did he run.

As he ran across the hard sands, he saw her dive to join the big seal who was waiting for her, and he gave a loud cry to stop her. For a moment she rested on the surface of the sea, then she cried with her voice that was like the waves singing in a shell, "Fare ye well, and all good befall you, for you were a good man to me."

Then she dived to the fairy places that lie at the bottom of the sea and the big seal with her.

For a long time her husband watched for her to come back to him and the children; but she came no more.

FRIEND SO-AND-SO, FRIEND SUCH-AND-SUCH

from

THE ARABIAN NIGHTS

retold by

NAOMI LEWIS

Though the scene of this sparkling tale belongs to old Arabia, elements of the plot may seem familiar to readers of western fairy lore. Here, especially, are the impossible tasks and the magic helper – what a helper too! But there are differences, both from the eastern and western kind that give a particular quality to the story. Unusually, both the fish-

erman and his wife, not to mention the obliging spirit ("that which was in the well") are real characters. Note too that it is the wife who solves the problem, never losing her delightful air of calm. How did she come to have such a helper? Has she some magical power herself? Answered or not, these intriguing questions tease us with off-stage mystery. With its wit, good humour and lively text, this is an ideal story for reading aloud, whatever the age of the listener.

L ong, long ago there lived in a city edged by the salt sea a fisherman, happily married to a very beautiful wife. But though he rose early and worked hard, he never earned more than would feed them for that one day. So that when he fell ill, there was no food in the house.

Next morning, his wife said, "If you cannot fish, we shall starve. If you can rise up now, I will carry your net and basket, and you can tell me what to do." The fisherman agreed, and slowly led the way to a stretch of shore at the foot of the Sultan's palace; it was known as a rich place for fishing. His wife came after, with basket and with net.

Now at that moment the Sultan was at his window, gazing out to sea. Suddenly he saw the fisherman's beautiful wife, and was seized with a longing to possess her. He called his Grand Wazir and asked for his advice.

"Shall I order the guards to kill the fisherman? Then I can marry the widow."

The wazir answered, "You cannot lawfully have the man put to death without a reason. Let me think. Ah, I have it. You know of course that the audience hall of the palace covers exactly an acre. I shall summon the fisherman and say that you command him, on pain of death, to cover the whole floor with a single piece of carpet. Since to do this is impossible, he can be disposed of without anyone suspecting a motive."

"Good, good," said the Sultan, rubbing his hands together.

So the wazir sent for the fisherman, and had him brought into the hall.

"O fisherman," he said, "our master, the king, requires you to cover this floor with a carpet, woven in a single piece. He allows you three days, and if you fail to produce the carpet, you shall be burnt in the fire. Write an agreement and seal it with your seal."

"What is all this?" said the fisherman. "I am not a man of carpets; I am a man of fish. Ask for any kind, size, colour of fish and I shall oblige, but – carpets? As Allah lives, I don't know them, and they don't know me. Fish, by all means. Carpets – no, no, no."

"Enough of your saucy words!" said the wazir. "The king has commanded this thing."

"Then seal it yourself," said the fisherman, and he ran from the palace in a great rage.

"Why are you so angry?" asked his wife.

"Be quiet, woman," he replied. "We have no time to waste. Bundle our clothes together, for we must flee from this city."

"But why?"

"Because the king means to kill me in three days' time."

"For what reason?" she persisted. So the fisherman told about the carpet.

"Oh, is that all?" she said. "Stop worrying. I will procure your carpet. Now, listen carefully. Go to the well in the garden, the one that is overlooked by a crooked tree. Put your head over the side and say, 'O So-and-so, your dear friend Such-and-such gives you greeting and begs you to send her the spindle which she forgot yesterday. We wish to carpet a room with it.'"

"You must be mad," said the fisherman, "but a desperate man tries anything."

He walked to the well and called down into it, "O So-and-so, your dear friend Such-and-such gives you greeting and begs you to send her the spindle which she forgot yesterday. We wish to carpet a room with it."

Then that which was in the well gave answer: "How could I refuse anything to my dear friend? Here is the spindle. When you have finished with it, bring it back to me." Up came a spindle; the fisherman neatly caught it and took it home.

"Good!" said his wife. "Now go to this tiresome wazir, and ask him for a large nail. Hammer this nail into the floor at one end of the hall, and fasten round it the end of the spindle thread. As you move away, the carpet will unfold itself behind you."

"People will think me mad," said the fisherman.

"Don't argue; do as I say," said the wife.

So the fisherman went with heavy steps to the palace, murmuring to himself, "O most unfortunate man! This is the last day of your life."

The Sultan and the wazir were waiting in the hall when he arrived.

"Well, where is the carpet?" said the Sultan.

"It is in my pocket," said the fisherman.

"Here is a fellow who jokes before his death," said the Sultan, laughing merrily, for soon he would gain his wish.

"Look here," said the fisherman, "you asked for a carpet. There the matter ends. If someone will fetch me a large nail, I can deal with the matter at once, and get on my way."

The wazir, still smiling, went to get the nail, and whispered to the Sultan's executioner, who was standing near the door, "As soon as you see that the fellow has no carpet, cut off his head without further orders."

The fisherman took the nail, hammered it in at the end of the hall, and fastened the thread to it. Then he took up the spindle, saying, "Spin my death; that's all you can do." But wait! a magnificent carpet began to flow out, covering the whole space of the floor with a weaving of marvellous beauty. The king and the wazir looked at each other in stunned silence. Then they whispered together.

Finally the wazir said, "Well, you've certainly done this task, and the king is satisfied. But he has another demand – easy enough for so smart a fellow as you. He requires you to bring him a little boy not more than eight days old, who shall tell him a story which is nothing but lies from beginning to end."

"Is that all?" said the fisherman bitterly. "That won't be difficult if you are so good as to bring me all today's newborn children of the Jinn."

"We do not want your jokes," said the wazir. "We think them in bad taste. You are allowed eight days to find the child, or your head will roll before our eyes in this very room. Write out an agreement and sign it with your seal."

"I know nothing about seals," said the fisherman, "nor of lying infants either. Fish – now that's another matter. I believe you want an excuse to get rid of me. Well, it may not be so easy."

He went home, and called out to his wife. "Hurry," he said. "Bundle our goods together – we must flee. I told you this before."

"But what happened about the carpet? Did the spindle work?"

"Oh yes, but now they want a little boy, less than eight days old, who will tell the Sultan a tale made of lies from beginning to end. They've given me eight days to find the creature."

"Don't worry," said his wife. "There's always a remedy."

But the eight days passed, and the fisherman still had no idea what to do. On the ninth morning he turned to his wife, saying, "Have you forgotten my problem? If you can do nothing, my life will end today."

"Don't worry so much," said the woman. "Go to the well beneath the twisted tree, give back the spindle with some grateful words, then add, 'O So-and-so, your dear friend Such-and-such begs you to lend her the boy who was born yesterday, for we need him in a certain matter.'" The fisherman went off grumbling that a two-day-old child would know even less than an eight-day one.

However, he returned the spindle and gave the message, adding, "And for Allah's sake be quick, for my head is just about to leave my shoulders!"

That which was in the well called up in answer, "Take the child and return it when the task is done." Up rose a swathed bundle which – Allah be praised! – he managed to catch before it fell back again.

As he made his way homeward, he thought to himself, "Even if this were an infant Jinnee, how could it speak, much less know enough truth to lie?" Aloud, he said, "Talk to me, child; I want to know if this is indeed the day of my death." The infant responded in the manner of its kind; it uttered tuneless wails and howls, and did that which soaked its wrappings, not sparing either the garments of the fisherman. The man was not pleased.

He said to his wife, "This infant has no wisdom; it utters nothing but noise, and it has ruined my clothes."

"Never mind about that," said his wife. "Just do what I tell you. When you reach the palace, be sure to demand three cushions for the child. Put one at each side of him and one at the back. And for good measure, utter a few prayers. They cost nothing and won't be wasted. Now be off."

When the wazir saw the fisherman arrive with the swaddled bundle, he swayed from side to side with laughter. Then he poked the child with a finger, but it did not speak, merely making the tuneless noise which all infants use as a voice.

The wazir ran to the king, crying joyfully, "The man has brought a newborn infant, and all it does is wail! Soon you will have your wish." Then the Sultan and the wazir made their way to the great hall, where the court had assembled, and the fisherman was called forth.

"First," said he, "I must have three cushions. Then you will hear what you will hear." The cushions were brought; the child was placed on a couch, and the fisherman used them as the wife had said to prop the child in an upright position. The king peered down.

"Is this thing the infant which is supposed to tell us a story made of lies?" he asked.

But before the fisherman could answer, the day-old child remarked, "Greeting, O king and company."

"Greeting to you," replied the astonished king. "Have you a story for us without a grain of truth?"

"Listen," said the child. "Once, when I was a young man, I bought a water melon for a hundred gold dinars because I was thirsty, and the fruit was cheap and plentiful. I cut it open and saw inside a tiny city. At once I stepped within, one leg at a time. For many hours I wandered through the shops and houses in the fruit. At last I stopped at a date tree, growing on a mountain top, each date at least a yard long. I climbed into the tree to gather some, but found it full of peasants sewing seeds of corn, and others harvesting, so quickly did the grain grow. I saw a train of little cocks and little hens; hand in hand, they were going off to get married. A donkey offered me a sesame cake, saying, 'Think before you eat.' I broke it in half and saw within the king and his wazir, busily whispering plots. They leapt out of the cake; I followed them briskly, and we all arrived this morning where you see us now."

"Enough!" cried the king. "O sheikh and crown of liars! There can't be a grain of truth in anything you have said."

The child replied, "I can speak truth as well. Shall I tell the court the reason why you persecute the fisherman? You wish to kill him because you saw his beautiful wife and you wish to possess her. Is this worthy of a mighty king? I swear by Allah that if you do not leave the man and his wife in peace from now onward, I shall wipe you out so thoroughly – you and your wazir too – that not even the flies will find a trace of your remains."

Having said these awful words, the infant turned to the fisherman. "Now, uncle," he demanded, "take me away from here." The people all stood back and made a path as the man and infant left, no one daring to speak. The child was returned to the well, with words of grateful thanks, and the fisherman and his delightful wife lived merrily together, untouched by harm, for years beyond this story.

THE PRINCESS AND THE PEA

by
HANS CHRISTIAN ANDERSEN

retold by
SUSAN PRICE

When Andersen, still a young man, had begun to make his name as a writer for adults (novels, plays, travel books), suddenly, perhaps for his own amusement – it's hard to say – he set down a few little tales of the folk and fairy kind. Four were published together as a small book in May 1835. One of them was "The Princess and the Pea" – the first, or nearly the first, in the great collection that was, in time, to follow. Like most of Andersen's earliest stories, it grew out of tales he had heard or

overheard as a child, often from women working at hop-gathering or in
the spinning room. But even at the start, his touch was unmistakable. As
you may see, he has done away with distance. You are out of the rain,
inside that homely palace. You can nod your head at the problem facing
the kindly royal couple. And the storyteller is speaking directly to you.

A few tales do exist of princes (or others) trying to prove their royal
sensitivity – in one, a hair replaces the pea. But Andersen's is the clas-
sic of the subject. It seems that a few early translators thought that one
pea was ridiculous, and added a few. If any such version comes your
way, remove those unworthy peas.

Once upon a time there was a Prince, and he wanted to marry a Princess; but she had to be a *real* Princess. He travelled all over the world in his search for a Princess, and Princesses he found in plenty; but whether they were *real* Princesses he couldn't decide, for now one thing, now another, seemed not quite right. At last he returned home to his palace and was very sad, because he wished so much to have a real Princess for his wife.

One evening there was a fearful storm; thunder crashed, lightning flashed, rain poured down from the sky in torrents – and it was dark as dark can be. All at once there was heard a knocking at the door. The Prince's father, the old King himself, went out to open it.

A Princess stood outside; but gracious! what a sight she was, out there in the rain. Water trickled down from her hair; water dripped from her clothes; water ran in at the toes of her shoes and out at the heels. And yet she said she was a real Princess.

"We shall soon see about that!" thought the old Queen, but she didn't say anything.

She went into the bedroom, took all the clothes off the bed and laid one dried pea on the mattress. Then she piled twenty more mattresses on top of it, and twenty eiderdowns over that. On this the girl who said she was a real Princess was to lie all night.

The next morning she was asked how she had slept.

"Oh, shockingly!" she replied. "I haven't even closed my eyes. I don't know what was in my bed, but there was something hard that has bruised me all over."

They saw at once that she must be a *real* Princess, for she had felt the little dried pea through twenty eiderdowns and twenty mattresses. Only a *real* Princess could have such delicate skin.

So the Prince asked the Princess to marry him, and the pea was put in a museum, as a curiosity. You may go yourself and see it.

Now, wasn't that a *real* story?

PUSS IN BOOTS

by
CHARLES PERRAULT

translated by
NAOMI LEWIS

*This well-liked story, with a number of other nursery favourites, comes from
the French of Charles Perrault. (For more of this interesting man, see the
Introduction.) His book of* Tales from Olden Times, with Moral Endings
*first appeared in English translation in 1729 and the lively Puss has been
with us ever since. Of course, it is the cat that we remember, the magic
helper who holds together all the absurdities of the plot: who cares for the
very ordinary jumped-up peasant boy prince? (But see the moral.) Allowing
for the fact that "Chat Botté" (the real Perrault title) was first told in
French, as you read you can almost hear the long-ago talker's kindly,
urbane voice, as he lets the plot carry him along, from scene to scene,
notion to notion, for his intently listening children. But once set down on
paper, his clear and elegant style, his eye for detail, his avoidance of the vulgar and the brutal, are unmistakable. His somewhat worldly moral verses
– very practical – show that he was not taken in by his characters. I have
added a verse of further comment, in, I hope, Perrault's mood.*

There was once a miller who lived and died a poor man. He had nothing to leave to his three sons but his mill, his ass and his cat. The sharing out was soon done: why call in a lawyer? The fees would have swallowed up those few legacies in a moment. So the oldest had the mill, the second the ass, and the third – can you guess? – the cat.

The third – the youngest brother – was not at all pleased. There he sat in the dumps. "If my brothers join forces," he sighed, "with a mill and an ass they can make an honest living. But what can I do? When I have eaten Puss here, and made a cap from his skin, I will just have to die of hunger."

The cat busily washed his paw, as if he were not listening, but he had taken in every word. Now, in a firm and serious voice, he spoke. "Stop moping, master. You are better off than you know. Just give me a little sack and a pair of boots in my size – the wood is full of thorns and briars – and you'll soon stop complaining about your legacy."

The young man did not feel too hopeful. What could a cat do to help? Then he began to think. This cat had always seemed unusually quick and intelligent. He remembered some of his cunning tricks to deceive the rats and mice inside the mill. He would hide in a sack of meal, or hang downwards from his feet, pretending to be dead – the creature was never short of ideas.

So Puss was fitted out with little boots and a bag tied with cords, which he hung around his neck. Straightway he went to a piece of waste ground that was full of rabbit warrens. He propped open the bag, put some tempting bran and lettuce leaves inside, stretched himself out on the ground as if he were dead, and waited for some young and innocent rabbit to find the treat.

The plan worked. He had scarcely lain down for a minute when something entered the bag – a little rabbit, not yet knowing the cunning ways of the world. Puss quickly drew the cords together to close the top, and set off.

Where did he go? To the royal palace, no less. Delighted with his catch, he asked to see the king. He was shown into a grand room where the king was sitting. The cat made a deep bow: "Your Majesty," he said, "I have here a gift for you, a fine rabbit from the estate of the Marquis of Carabas. He has sent me here to present it to you on his behalf."

"Tell your master," said the king, "that I thank him, and am pleased to accept his gift."

A few days later Puss went and hid in a cornfield; using his bag as before he caught two partridges. Promptly he went to the palace and presented them to the king with the same message: an offering from the lands of the Marquis of Carabas. Again, the king was pleased to accept, and this time gave the bringer a gold coin for himself.

For the next three months the cat continued this game, bringing to the king some gift from his wealthy master's estate – well, that was the cat's story! One day, when he knew that the king was taking a drive by the river with his daughter – the most beautiful girl in the world, I must tell you – Puss said to his master: "Now, if you do exactly what I say, your fortune is made. You have only to go for a swim in the river – I will show you where – then leave the rest to me."

The young man obeyed the cat's instructions, though he could not imagine what good it could do him. As soon as he was in the water, Puss began to cry out at the top of his voice, "Help! Help! The Marquis of Carabas is drowning!" The king heard the noise, looked out of the carriage window, recognised the cat-messenger, bringer of all the presents, and ordered his guard to go to the rescue of the noble Marquis.

While they were pulling the very wet young man from the river, the cat rushed to the carriage, saying, "Your Majesty! While my master was in the water, robbers came and stole his clothes. He cried out, 'Stop thief! Stop thief!' But the villains got away." The king at once ordered his royal wardrobe officers to bring out their finest clothes for the Marquis of Carabas.

The young man was a handsome fellow in his own right. Splendidly dressed, he certainly looked as a noble lord in a fairy tale should look. The king greeted him as if he were his closest friend. The king's daughter – well, she admired him too, and after receiving several respectful but far from indifferent glances from the handsome stranger, she fell deeply in love with him.

The king now invited him into the royal carriage. "You must join us," he said, "in our drive through the countryside."

Puss was thrilled to see his plan succeeding so well, but there was still much to be done. He raced on ahead, and seeing some peasants mowing a cornfield he said to them, "My good fellows, I have some news for you. The king is about to pass. You are to tell him that these fields belong to the Marquis of Carabas. If you don't, then every one of you will be chopped into mincemeat."

The king soon reached the field. "Who owns this land?" he asked.

"The Marquis of Carabas," the mowers answered together. The cat's threat had terrified them.

"You have some fine meadow-land," said the king to the young man.

"Your Majesty," replied the miller's son, "this meadow never fails to produce a wonderful crop, year after year." The cat's master had become a good pupil to his cat.

Again the clever Puss went on ahead, and this time came to a field with harvesters. "My good fellows," he said. "I have some news for you. The king is just coming past. You will tell him that this land belongs to the Marquis of Carabas – yes? If you don't, you will all be chopped into mincemeat."

A few minutes later the royal carriage reached the field. "And who is the owner of this land?" asked the king.

"The Marquis of Carabas," the peasants replied in chorus. Again the king congratulated the young man. The cat continued to go ahead, telling the field workers what they must say, and the king was quite amazed at the vast possessions of the Marquis of Carabas.

At last, the cat reached a great castle. It belonged to an ogre, the richest ever known; indeed, all the lands that the king had just passed through were his. The cat had already made some enquiries about the ogre, and now he asked the gatekeeper if his master would allow him the honour of a visit. "It would not be polite to pass the magnificent place without paying homage to its owner."

The ogre received him as civilly as an ogre could, and told him that he could sit down. "I have heard reports of your wonderful power," said Puss, after thanking him, "and some I find hard to believe. They say, for instance, that you can change into any kind of animal—an elephant, a lion even."

"It's quite true," said the ogre gruffly, "and to prove it, you are just about to see me become a lion. GR-R-R-R! GR-R-R-R!" And there, in place of the ogre, was a monstrous lion! Puss was so frightened that he leapt onto the roof. This was none too easy; his boots weren't meant for walking on tiles.

At last, when he was quite sure that the ogre had returned to his own shape, Puss came down, and confessed that he had been very alarmed indeed. "However," he continued, "I have also been told that you turn into a very small animal – a rat, say, or a mouse. Now that, I must confess, seems to me impossible."

"Impossible?" said the ogre. "Just watch!" And at once there was no ogre any more, only a tiny mouse, which went skittering over the floor. The next moment Puss had pounced upon the mouse and devoured it.

And only just in time, for the royal carriage had reached the castle. "What a magnificent building!" said the king. "We must have a closer view." The cat was always ready for emergencies. As soon as he heard the carriage rumble over the drawbridge, he ran forward and said to the king, "Welcome, Your Majesty, to the castle of the Marquis of Carabas!"

"Can this be?" said the king. "Is this really yours as well? I am amazed. Well, from the outside I have never seen anything finer. Now, if you please, let us see the interior."

The king went first, the miller's son followed, taking the hand of the young princess, and they entered the great hall. There they found a delicious meal set out. The ogre had been expecting friends to dinner, but the guests, seeing the king's carriage, had been afraid to enter and had gone away. The king himself was now completely overcome by the wealth and charm of the young Marquis. His daughter, too, he noted, was already madly in love with the handsome fellow. So, after tossing down several cups of wine, he turned to his host and said, "Well, Marquis, the decision is yours. Do you wish to be my son-in-law?"

The miller's son bowed low. "I accept the honour most happily," he replied. That very same day the two young people were married.

The cat was given a title and a high position in the palace. He never needed to chase a mouse again. If he did so well, it was just for exercise, or for his own amusement.

MORAL

"Reader, are you waiting still
For a rich relation's will?
Wealth's not all you can inherit
Money's fine, but so is merit.
Enterprise, imagination,
Quick wit, sense and concentration
Can lift you to the highest reaches –
So this story seems to teach us."

Here, Monsieur Perrault paused and smiled.
"It's true," he said, "a clever child,
Will note – these virtues were the cat's,
Though master had the benefits."
With Puss at hand, how could he fail?
But his was the luck of fairy tale.
Today, such cats are few, alas;
Still, there's a road to Carabas.
And what's the way of finding it?
Be diligent, and don't omit
To use (like Puss) resource and wit.

ANOTHER MORAL

If a miller's son can please
And win a princess with such ease
Where can you find a moral?
Except to say, it does no harm
To have good looks, and youth and charm –
and who with that would quarrel?

THE TROLL BRIDE

by
SUSAN PRICE

Trolls, like elves and fairies, humans too, can be good or bad or some-thing in between. These kinds are all within this book. They are odd to look at, certainly, not unlike the gnarled forest trees and craggy rocks that are their haunts. If trolls are what you seek, you must go north; Scandinavia is their chosen home. The throwing over the church in this splendid tale may be an echo of an old Danish legend. But Susan Price, a notably gifted writer, remains a real original while entering freely into legend-country and speaking its language like a native. If you doubt this, read her awesome novel The Ghost Drum. *Read it anyway. The cheerful and witty "Troll Bride" is lighter, to be sure, but it is still unmistakably Price. One of its many points of interest is the reversal of the usual Beauty-and-Beast situation. In the case of this devoted couple, the unpretty one of the two (but nice) is the lady. Don't overlook the final sentence.*

Once, in Denmark, there was a young man who married a troll's daughter, a fine, strapping girl, much taller than he was, with tremendous shoulders and forearms, a head of golden hair stiffer than gold wire, and a long, strong tail which she wagged when she saw him. They married because they each felt perfectly suited to the other, and they were very happy together; but the people of the young man's village were not pleased at all. "What sort of marriage-service was that?" they said. "'Do you take this man? – Do you take this troll?' That can't be right."

"Did you see how much the thing ate after the service?" others said. "Give it a week or two, and it'll be eating *him*."

Most often the villagers said, "What *can* he see in it?"

They were so suspicious of the troll bride that none of them would have anything to do with her, even though she tried hard to be friendly. The village children, who had been told that she would eat them, threw stones after her, called her names, and then ran from her in a panic; the women she spoke to turned their backs on her; and the men shied away from her as they might from a bear. They made her very unhappy; and even though her husband appealed to them to be kinder to her, they refused. "You wait," they told him, "until it shows its *real* nature." He went angrily back to his troll bride then, swearing that he would have nothing more to do with his own people.

One Sunday, while the villagers were in church, the troll

bride's father, a huge old troll with stiff black hair and a black beard, came to the barn where the newly-married couple were living until the husband could build a house large enough for his wife. The old troll had travelled down from the mountains to visit his daughter and find out if she was happy. When he heard how the villagers were treating her, he was angry. He scowled so that his brows covered his eyes; he showed his long teeth; he lashed his tail. To his daughter, he said, "Will you throw or catch?"

"Oh Father," she said. "You won't hurt the poor little things?"

"Will you throw or catch?" repeated the big old troll, his hair bristling.

"I'll catch, Father," she said.

"Then come along," said the troll, and he left the barn, his daughter and much smaller son-in-law following.

The troll led them up the hill to the churchyard, where they waited, and listened to the murmur of prayers and the singing of hymns from inside the church. The service ended, the people came out – and crowded back into the church at the sight of an even bigger, fiercer and more frightening troll than the one they were already plagued with.

"Go round to the other side of the building, daughter," said the troll, and, when she had, he beckoned to the people inside the church. Some of them went out to him, too afraid to do anything but obey; others were pushed out by the priest, who was afraid that the troll would destroy his church to reach them if he did not. The troll picked them up one by one, and threw them over the church roof. They howled as they rushed upward, and flapped their arms, trying to fly; but it was worse when they felt themselves beginning to fall. Then their shrieks and moans were so comical that some of the villagers still on the ground couldn't help giggling, until the troll picked them up.

On the other side of the church the troll's daughter caught them as they came tumbling towards her, set them safely on their feet, straightened their clothes, and patted their heads. When her father had thrown every one of them – except his son-in-law – over the roof, he came round the corner of the building and found them all standing, sitting or lying about his daughter's skirts, all shaking hard enough to shake off their clothes.

"If I ever again hear that you have made my daughter unhappy," said the troll, "we shall play this game once more; but on that day, she will throw, and *I* will catch. Do you understand me, people?"

All the villagers understood him very well, and as soon as the troll had gone back to the mountains, everyone in the village began calling on the troll bride, to give her eggs and cakes, and helpful hints; and everyone who met her wished her good morning and smiled; and the villagers soon discovered that, despite her fierce appearance, she was kind and gentle, and eager to please. They forgot everything unkind they had said about her when she arrived, and went about telling each other that they had thought from the first day that she was a "lovely thing". Before long the troll bride was gossiping with the neighbours every day, helping with embroidery and knitting in the evenings, and minding children. She was happier than she had ever been, but her husband, who hardly ever saw her any more, was somewhat bitter.

RAPUNZEL

by
THE BROTHERS GRIMM
retold by
LORE SEGAL

The plot of Rapunzel, if you look into it, is made up of several familiar elements: an infant promised to a witch or sorcerer in return for a needed favour or unrealised theft; a girl shut in a tower; the usual (nameless) prince; a forest . . . And yet, allied together, they make a story that, once heard, stays always in the mind. Why? Well, first, I think, the name itself: Rapunzel. Few fairy tale characters do have names, and this one is curiously memorable. Then, the heroine's long, long golden hair, which serves both witch and prince as a ladder to her tower. Rapunzel herself, as so often in fairy tale, is a simple, rather passive creature, pushed to and fro by chance and magic, a victim right from the start. But visually and dramatically she somehow achieves real heroine status. You may not know that most earlier versions chose to leave out the fact that Rapunzel, after meeting the prince, gave birth to twins. You will find them here.

Once upon a time there was a man and wife who had long wished for a child. Finally the woman was filled with hope and expected God would grant her wish. The couple had a little window at the back of their house and you could look down into a magnificent garden full of the loveliest flowers and herbs. But the garden was surrounded by a high wall and nobody dared go in because it belonged to a great and powerful witch who was feared by all the world. One day the woman was standing by the window looking into the garden and saw a bed planted with the most beautiful lettuce, of the kind they call Rapunzel. It looked so fresh and green that she began to crave it and longed fiercely to taste the lettuce. Each day her longing grew and because she knew she could not have it, she began to pine and look pale and miserable. Her husband got frightened and said, "Dear wife, are you ill?" "Ah," said she, "if I cannot have some lettuce from the garden behind our house, I will die." The husband loved her very much, and said to himself, You can't let your wife die; fetch her some lettuce, whatever the cost may be. In the evening, therefore, at twilight, he clambered over the wall into the witch's garden, hurriedly dug up a handful of lettuce, and brought it home to his wife, and she made herself a salad right away and ate it ravenously. It tasted good, oh so good that the next day she craved it three times as much. If she was to have any peace, her husband must climb into the garden once again. And so at twilight he went back, but when he got down the other side of the wall he stood horrified, for there, standing right in front of him, was the witch. "How dare you come climbing into my garden, stealing my lettuce like a thief?" said she, and her eyes were angry. "You shall pay for this!" "Ah, no, please," cried the man. "Let justice be tempered with mercy! Only my despair made me do what I did. My wife saw your lettuce out of our window and felt such a craving that she had to have some, or die." And so the witch's anger began to cool and she said, "If that is so, I will allow you to take as much lettuce as you want on one condition: You must give me the child your wife brings into the world. It shall be well cared for. I will look after it like a mother." In his terror the man agreed to everything and no sooner had the wife been brought to bed than the witch appeared. She named the child Rapunzel and took it away with her.

Rapunzel grew into the most beautiful child under the sun. When she was twelve years old, the witch locked her up in a tower that stood in the forest and had neither stair nor door, only way at the top there was a little window. If the witch wanted to get inside, she came and stood at the bottom and called:

> *"Rapunzel, Rapunzel,*
> *Let down your hair."*

Rapunzel had magnificent long hair, fine as spun gold. Now when she heard the voice of the witch, she unfastened her braids, wound them around a hook on the window, and let the hair fall twenty feet to the ground below, and the witch climbed up.

After some years it happened that the king's son rode through the forest, past the tower, and heard singing so lovely he stood still and listened. It was Rapunzel in her loneliness, who made the time pass by letting her sweet voice ring through the forest. The prince wanted to climb up the tower and looked for the door but could not find one. So he rode home, but the singing had so moved his heart he came back to the forest day after day and listened. Once, when he was standing there behind a tree, he saw how a witch came along and heard her calling:

"Rapunzel, Rapunzel,
Let down your hair."

And then Rapunzel let her braids down and the witch climbed up. "If that's the ladder one takes to the top, I'll try my luck too." Next day, when it began to get dark, he went to the tower and called:

"Rapunzel, Rapunzel,
Let down your hair."

And the hair was let down and the prince climbed up.

At first Rapunzel was very much frightened when a man stepped in, because her eyes had never seen anything like him before, but the prince spoke very kindly to her and told her how his heart had been so moved by her singing he had wanted to see her. And so Rapunzel lost her fear, and when he asked her if she would take him for her husband and she saw how young and beautiful he was, she thought, He will love me better than my old godmother, and said, "Yes," and put her hand in his hand. She said, "I would like to go with you but I don't know how to get down from here. Every time you come, bring a skein of silk with you. I will braid a ladder and when the ladder is finished I will climb down and you will take me on your horse." Until that time the prince was to come to her every evening, for by day came the old woman. The witch knew nothing about all this until one day Rapunzel opened her mouth and said, "Tell me, Godmother, why is it you are so much harder to pull up than the young prince? He's with me in the twinkling of an eye." "Oh, wicked child!" cried the witch. "What is this! I thought I had kept you from all the world and still you deceive me," and in her fury she grasped Rapunzel's lovely hair, wound it a number of times around her left hand, and with her right hand seized a pair of scissors and snip snap, the beautiful braids lay on the floor. And so pitiless was she that she took poor Rapunzel into a wilderness and left her there to live in great misery and need.

On the evening of the day on which she had banished Rapunzel, the witch tied the severed braids to the hook at the window, and when the prince came and called:

"Rapunzel, Rapunzel,
Let down your hair,"

she let the hair down. The prince climbed up and found not his dearest Rapunzel but the witch looking at him with her wicked, venomous eyes. "Ah, ha," cried she mockingly, "you come to fetch your ladylove, but the pretty bird has flown the nest and stopped singing. The cat's got it and will scratch out your eyes too. You have lost Rapunzel and will never see her again." The prince was beside himself with grief and in his despair jumped out of the tower. His life was saved but he had fallen into thorns that pierced his eyes. And so he stumbled blindly about the forest, living on roots and berries, and did nothing but wail and weep for the loss of his dearest wife. And so for years he wandered in misery; finally he came into the wilderness where Rapunzel lived meagrely with her twin children, a boy and a girl, whom she had brought into the world. He heard her voice and it sounded so familiar to him. He walked towards it and Rapunzel recognized him and fell around his neck and cried. Two of her tears moistened his eyes and they regained their light and he could see as well as ever. He took her to his kingdom, where he was received with joy, and they lived happily and cheerfully for many years to come.

VASILISSA, BABA YAGA, AND THE LITTLE DOLL

by

ALEXANDER AFANASIEV

retold by

NAOMI LEWIS

In this magnificent story you will meet the greatest witch in all tradi-
tional fairy tale, the Russian Baba Yaga. (For some thoughts on the
"invented" kind, see the Introduction.) She is almost alone in having a
name. Her home is like none other – a hut mounted on hens' claws; it
moves to her needs and wishes. She rides the air in – of all things – a
mortar, whose wildly waving pestle serves as oar. In her service are the
three mighty horsemen, Morning, Noon and Night, the white, the red
and the black riders on their matching steeds. She is indestructible; she
survives every tale in which she appears. And in her own, grim way, she
has a kind of humour, and plays fair with our heroine. She can even
appreciate the skill of another magic worker (the doll). After all, who
wins? Who, if anyone, loses? A good question.

In a far-off land in a far-off time, on the edge of a great forest, lived a girl named Vasilissa. Ah, poor Vasilissa! She
was no more than eight years old when her mother died.
But she had a friend, and that one was better than most. Who
was this friend? A doll. As the mother lay ill she had called the
child to her bedside. "Vasilissa," she said, "here is a little doll.
Take good care of her, and whenever you are in great need, give
her some food and ask for her help; she will tell you what to do.
Take her, with my blessing; but remember, she is your secret;
no one else must know of her at all. Now I can die content."

The father of Vasilissa grieved for a time, then married a new
wife, thinking that she would care for the little girl. But did she
indeed! She had two daughters of her own, and not one of the
three had a grain of love for Vasilissa. From early dawn to the
last light of day, in the hot sun or the icy wind, they kept her toil-
ing at all the hardest tasks, in or out of the house; never did she

have a word of thanks. Yet whatever they set her to do was done, and done in time. For when she truly needed help she would set her doll on a ledge or table, give her a little food and drink, and tell the doll her troubles. With her help all was done.

One day in the late autumn the father had to leave for the town, a journey of many days. He set off at earliest dawn.

Darkness fell early. Rain beat on the cottage windows; the wind howled down the chimney – just the time for the wife to work a plan she had in mind. To each of the girls she gave a task: the first was set to making lace, the second to knitting stockings, Vasilissa to spinning.

"No stirring from your place, my girls, before you have done," said the woman. Then, leaving them a single candle, she went to bed.

The three worked on for a while, but the light was small, and flickered. One sister pretended to trim the wick and it went out altogether – just as the mother had planned.

"Now we're in trouble," said the girl. "For where's the new light to come from?"

"There's only one place," said her sister, "and that's from Baba Yaga."

"That's right," said the other. "But who's to go?

> *"My needles shine;*
> *The job's not mine."*

"I can manage too," said the other.

> *"My lace-pins shine;*
> *The job's not mine.*

Vasilissa must go."

"Yes, Vasilissa must go!" they cried together. And they pushed her out of the door.

Now who was Baba Yaga? She was a mighty witch; her hut was set on claws, like the legs of giant hens. She rode in a mortar over the highest mountains, speeding it on with the pestle, sweeping away her traces with a broom. And she would crunch up in a trice any human who crossed her path.

But Vasilissa had a friend, and that one better than most. She took the doll from her pocket, and set some bread before her. "Little doll," she said, "they are sending me into the forest to fetch a light from Baba Yaga's hut – and who has ever returned from there? Help me, little doll."

The doll ate, and her eyes grew bright as stars. "Have no fear," said she. "While I am with you nothing can do you harm. But remember – no one else must know of your secret. Now let us start."

How dark it was in the forest of towering trees! How the leaves hissed, how the branches creaked and moaned in the wind! But Vasilissa walked resolutely on, hour after hour. Suddenly, the earth began to tremble and a horseman thundered by. Both horse and rider were glittering white, hair and mane, swirling cloak and bridle too; and as they passed, the sky showed the first white light of dawn.

Vasilissa journeyed on, then again she heard a thundering noise, and a second horse and rider flashed into sight. Both shone red as scarlet, red as flame, swirling cloak and bridle too; as they rode beyond her view, the sun rose high. It was day.

On she walked, on and on, until she reached a clearing in

the woods. In the centre was a hut – but the hut had feet; and they were the claws of hens. It was Baba Yaga's home, no doubt about that. All around was a fence of bones, and the posts were topped with skulls: a fearful sight in the fading light! And as she gazed, a third horseman thundered past; but this time horse and rider were black and black, swirling cloak and bridle too. They vanished into the gloom, and it was night. But, as darkness fell, the eyes of the skulls lit up like lamps and everything in the glade could be seen as sharp as day.

Swish! Swoosh! Varoom! Varoom! As Vasilissa stood there, frozen stiff with fear, a terrible noise came from over the forest. The wind screeched, the leaves hissed – Baba Yaga was riding home in her huge mortar, using her pestle as an oar, sweeping away the traces with her broom. At the gate of the hut she stopped and sniffed the air with her long nōse.

"Phoo! Phoo! I smell Russian flesh!" she croaked. "Who's there? Out you come!"

Vasilissa took courage, stepped forward and made a low curtsey.

"It is I, Vasilissa. My sisters sent me for a light, since ours went out."

"Oh, so that's it!" said the witch. "I know those girls, and their mother too. Well, nothing's for nothing, as they say; you must work for me for a while, then we'll see about the light." She turned to the hut and sang in a high shrill screech:

> *"Open gates! Open gates!*
> *Baba Yaga waits."*

The weird fence opened; the witch seized the girl's arm in

her bony fingers and pushed her into the hut. "Now," said she, "get a light from the lamps outside," – she meant the skulls – "and serve my supper. It's in the oven, and the soup's in the cauldron there." She lay down on a bench while Vasilissa carried the food to the table until she was quite worn out, but she dared not stop. And the witch devoured more than ten strong men could have eaten – whole geese and hens and roasted pigs; loaf after loaf; huge buckets of beer and wine, cider and Russian kvass. At last, all that remained was a crust of bread.

"There's your supper, girl," said the witch. "But you must earn it, mind; I don't like greed. While I'm off tomorrow I must clear out the yard; it hasn't been touched for years, and it quite blocks out the view. Then you must sweep the hut, wash the linen, cook the dinner – and mind you cook enough; I was half-starved tonight. Then – for I'll have no lazybones around – there's another little job. You see that sack? It's full of black beans, wheat and poppy seed, some other things too, I dare say. Sort them out into their separate lots, and if a single one is out of place, woe betide! Into the cauldron you shall go, and I'll crunch you up for breakfast in a trice."

So saying, she lay down by the stove and was instantly fast asleep. Snorrre . . . Snorrre . . . It was a horrible sound.

Vasilissa took the doll from her pocket and gave her the piece of bread. "Little doll," said she. "How am I to do all these tasks? Or even one of them? How can a little doll like you help now? We are lost indeed."

"Vasilissa," said the doll. "Again I tell you, have no fear.

Say your prayers and go to sleep. Tomorrow knows what is hidden from yesterday."

She slept – but she woke early, before the first glimmer of day. Where should she start on the mountain of work? Then she heard a thundering of hoofs; white horse and white rider flashed past the window – suddenly it was dawn. The light in the skulls' eyes dwindled and went out. Then the poor girl hid in the shadows, for she saw Baba Yaga get to her feet – Creak! Creak! – and shuffle to the door. There, the witch gave a piercing whistle, and mortar, pestle and broom came hurtling towards her, stopping where she stood. In she stepped, off she rode, over tree-tops, through the clouds, using the pestle like an oar, sweeping away her traces with the broom. Just as she soared away, the red horse and red rider thundered past: suddenly it was day, and the sun shone down.

Vasilissa turned away from the window, but what was this? She could not believe her eyes.

Every task was done. The yard was cleared, the linen washed, the grains and the seeds were all in separate bins, the dinner was set to cook. And there was the little doll, waiting to get back in her pocket. "All you need to do," said the doll, "is to set the table and serve it all, hot and hot, when she returns. But keep your wits about you all the same, for she's a sly one."

The winter daylight faded fast; again there was a thundering of hoofs; black horse, black rider sped through the glade and were gone. Darkness fell, and the eyes of the skulls once more began to glow. And then, with a swish and a roar, down swept the mortar, out stepped Baba Yaga.

"Well, girl, why are you standing idle? You know what I told you."

"The work is all done, granny."

Baba Yaga looked and looked but done it all was. So she sat down, grumbling and mumbling, to eat her supper. It was good, very good: it put her in a pleasant humour, for a witch.

"Tell me, girl, why do you sit there as if you were dumb?"

"Granny, I did not dare to speak – but, now, if you permit it, may I ask a question?"

"Ask if you will, but remember that not every question leads to good. The more you know, the older you grow."

"Well, granny, can you tell me, who is the white rider on the white horse, the one who passed at dawn?"

"He is my Bright Morning, and he brings the earliest light."

"Then who is the rider all in red on the flame-red horse?"

"Ah, he is my Fiery Sun and brings the day."

"And who is the horseman all in black on the coal-black horse?"

"He is my Dark Night. All are my faithful servants. Now I shall ask *you* a question; mind you answer me properly. How did you do all those tasks I set you?"

Vasilissa recalled her mother's words, never to tell the secret of the doll.

"My mother gave me a blessing before she died, and that helps me when in need."

"A blessing! I want no blessed children here! Out you get! Away! Away!" And she pushed her through the door. "You've earned your pay – now take it." She took down one of the gate-post skulls, fixed it on a stick, and thrust it into Vasilissa's hand. "Now – off!"

Vasilissa needed no second bidding. She hastened on, her path now lit by the eyes of the fearful lamp. And so, at last, she was home.

"Why have you taken so long?" screamed the mother and the sisters. They had been in darkness ever since she left. They had gone in every direction to borrow a light, but once it was inside in the house, every flame went out. So they seized the skull with joy.

But the glaring eyes stared back; wherever they turned they could not escape the scorching rays. Soon, all that remained of the three was a little ash. Then the light of the skull went out for ever; its task was done.

Vasilissa buried it in the garden, and a bush of red roses sprang up on the spot. She did not fear to be alone, for the little doll kept her company. And when her father returned, rejoicing to see her, this tale she told him, just as it has been told to you.

THE FLYING TRUNK

by

HANS CHRISTIAN ANDERSEN

translated by

NAOMI LEWIS

This is a fairly early Andersen story (1839), but a significant one. It brings together the writer who, like most later authors in this field, drew on familiar fairy tale plots, and the genius, the real original who had discovered that there was no need for this. Everything around had a story: an eggshell, a toy, a flower, a saucepan. The main idea of the present tale came, he explained, from the Arabian Nights, *with its magic carpet and flying horse, yet the trunk itself belongs to the "new" Andersen. He was always travelling, and as he wrote, his own old trunk must have caught his eye as it waited for its next journey.*

But there is more to the tale than that. The story within the story – the one that beguiled the King and Queen – is the inventive Andersen at his best. One of his great contributions to story was to show that things are characters in their own right. Well, aren't they? There's an enjoyable moment when the pot ("clean and refined") has told her story. Then "the broom took some parsley from the dustbin and put it round the pot like a crown; he knew that this would annoy the others. 'If I crown her today,' he thought, 'she will crown me tomorrow.'" I have to say that the end of the main tale is teasing. Did they find each other at last? Maybe. What's your opinion?

There was once a merchant who was so rich that he could have paved the whole street with silver, and still have had nearly enough over for a little alley-way as well. But that isn't what he did with his money – Oh no, he had more sense. Whenever he laid out a penny it brought him ten: that's the kind of merchant he was. And then he died.

All his money now came to his son – and he lost no time in spending it. Every night he went out dancing; he made paper kites from bank-notes; he played ducks and drakes on the lake – not with flat stones, but with gold coins. That's the way to run through money, and very soon he had nothing left but four copper coins and the clothes he had on, which were an old dressing gown and a pair of slippers. Needless to say, his friends all drifted off: who would wish to be seen with such a ragamuffin? But one of them, more good-natured than the rest, gave him an old trunk, saying,

"You'll be moving off, I fancy. That's for your luggage."

All very well, but he had no luggage. So he put himself in the trunk.

It was no ordinary trunk. As soon as you pressed the lock, it rose from the ground and flew. The young man pressed the lock and – swoosh! – the trunk was taking him up through the chimney, over the clouds, higher and higher, further and further away. The bottom creaked and groaned – what if it fell out? No acrobatics could help him then. But the trunk held together, and landed at last in the country of the Turks. He hid it under some leaves in a wood, and walked towards the town.

Nobody took any notice of him because all the Turks go about in dressing gowns and slippers. He met a nursemaid with a young child. "I say, nanny," he called out, "what's the great palace just outside the city, with the windows so high in the walls?"

"Oh, that's where the king's daughter lives," she answered. "A fortune-teller has prophesied that she's going to have an unhappy love-affair. So no one is allowed to visit her unless the king and queen are there as well."

"Thank you," said the merchant's son. He hurried back to the wood, stepped into his trunk and flew up, on to the palace roof. Then he climbed through the window of the princess's room. It was quite easy!

She was fast asleep on a sofa, and looked so beautiful that the merchant's son couldn't help giving her a kiss. This woke her up. Oh, she was frightened to see a strange man bending over her. But he explained that he was a Turkish god, and had come flying down from the sky to call on her. She liked that story.

Then they sat side by side, and he told her tales about her eyes: they were deep and lovely lakes, he said, and her thoughts swam through them like mermaids. He told her about her forehead; it was a snowy mountain, but inside were wonderful rooms and galleries, with the loveliest pictures on the walls. And he told her about the stork, which flies in with charming little babies – tales of that kind. And then he asked her to marry him, and she said yes.

"But you must come here on Saturday," she said. "That's when my parents, the king and queen, will be having tea with me. They *will* be proud that I am going to marry a Turkish god. But do be sure to tell them some good stories; they'll enjoy that so much. Only, my mother likes tales with a moral, very proper, you know, while Father prefers something lively, to make him laugh."

"Very well," said the merchant's son. "A story shall be my wedding present."

So they parted, but the princess gave him a sword which was decorated with gold coins. He had plenty of use for those.

Off he flew, and bought himself a new dressing gown. Then he sat down in the wood to think about his story. It had to be ready by Saturday, and that isn't so easy. But at last it was finished, and Saturday had arrived.

The king and queen and all the court were at the tea party, waiting for him to come. They gave him a charming welcome.

"Now, do tell us a story," said the queen. "But mind, it must have a serious moral."

"Yes, yes, but you must make us laugh as well," said the king.

"I'll do my best," said the young man, and he began his story. "Now, listen carefully.

"Once upon a time there was a bundle of matches. They were extremely proud and haughty because they came of such high beginnings. Their family tree – the one they had all been part of – was once a tall and ancient pine tree in the forest. Now the matches lay on a kitchen shelf between a tinder box and an old iron pot, and they told these neighbours all about the time when they were young.

"'Ah yes,' they said, 'we were on the top of the world when we were on that tree. Every morning and evening we had diamond tea – they call it dew – and all day we had sunshine (when there *was* any sunshine) and all the little birds had to tell us stories. We could easily see that we were grander than the rest; we could afford green clothes all the year round, while the poor oaks and beeches wore leaves only in summer time . . .

"'But then the woodcutter came – we call it the Great Revolution – and the family was split up. Our mighty trunk found a place as the mainmast of a great ship which could sail round the world if she'd a mind to. Jobs of various kinds were found for the branches, and we were appointed to bring light to the lower orders. You must be wondering how such high-born persons as ourselves came to be in this kitchen. Now you know.'

"'I have a different history,' said the iron pot. 'Ever since I first came into the world I have been scrubbed and boiled, boiled and scrubbed – I can't count the number of times. I do the solid work here, the only kind that matters. Strictly speaking, I'm the Number One person in this house. What do I most enjoy? I'll tell you. It's to settle down on this shelf, clean and tidy, when all the business of dinner is over, and have a sensible chat with friends. Except for the water-bucket, which goes into the yard now and then, we all prefer to stay at home. None of that foreign travel for us. The only one who brings in news is the shopping basket. But it's wild, disagreeable stuff, always about the government and the people. Why! Only the other day an elderly jug in this kitchen was so shaken by what the basket said that he fell down and broke into pieces. Yes, he was absolutely shattered. Yes, she's a real trouble-maker, that basket; I wouldn't trust her politics at all.'

"'You do ramble on,' growled the tinder box, and it clashed its flint and steel to give out sparks. 'I was hoping for a livelier evening.'

"'Yes,' said the matches, 'we do need brightening up. What about discussing which of us comes from the best family? That would be interesting.'

"'No, I don't like talking about myself,' said an earthenware pot. 'Let's do something more entertaining. For a start I'll tell you a story, the kind we can all enter into. Right? On the Baltic shores, where the Danish beech trees wave their boughs—'

"'What a fine beginning!' said the plates. 'We like that story already.'

"'Well,' continued the earthenware pot, 'it was there that I spent my youth, in a very respectable household. The furniture was polished every week, the floors washed every day, and clean curtains were put up every fortnight.'

"'You make it all sound so interesting,' said the broom. 'Anyone can tell you're a lady. Your story is so clean and refined.'

"'Yes, I thought that too,' said the water bucket, and it gave a hop and skip of pleasure, plink! plop! – on the kitchen floor. The pot went on with her story, and the end was just as good as the beginning. The plates all clattered together – that was their way of showing applause – while the broom took some parsley from the dustbin and put it round the pot like a crown; he knew that this would annoy the others. 'If I crown her today,' he thought, 'she'll crown me tomorrow.'

"'Now I'm going to dance,' said the tongs, and dance she did. My, my, how high she could kick her legs! The old chintz chair cover split right down the middle trying to get a good view. 'Where's my crown?' the tongs demanded when the dance was done. So she was crowned as well.

"'A common, vulgar lot,' thought the matches, but they kept the thought to themselves.

"The big tea-urn was asked to sing, but she had a cold, she said; unless she was on the boil she wasn't in good voice. The truth was that she was too conceited and proud to sing in the kitchen. She would only perform in the dining-room when the master and mistress were present.

"Over on the window ledge was an old quill pen that the

maid servant used. There was nothing special about her except the fact that she had been dipped too deep in the inkwell. This seemed to the pen a mark of distinction, and she was quite vain about it. 'If the tea-urn doesn't wish to sing,' said the pen, 'why should we try to make her? There's a nightingale outside; she can manage a few notes. It's true that she has never had lessons – the bird is quite uneducated – but let's not be fussy tonight.'

"'I don't approve at all,' said the kettle. She was the kitchen's chief vocalist; she was also half-sister to the tea-urn. 'Why should we listen to a foreign bird? Is it patriotic? I put it to the shopping-basket – don't you think I am right?'

"'I'm really disappointed,' said the basket. 'Is this the proper way to spend an evening, squabbling and squabbling? Wouldn't it be better to set our house in order? Let us start by putting everyone in his or her proper place. That, of course, will set me at the top; I'll be in charge. You'll see a few changes!'

"'Yes, why not?' said the dishes. 'We could do with a little stirring up.'

"But at that moment the door opened. It was the maid. Not one of them moved; not one of them made a sound. Yet every single pot in the place was silently telling itself how gifted it really was, how much above the rest in style and quality. 'Given the chance,' each thought, 'I could have made a real success of the evening.'

"The maid picked up the matches and struck them. How they spluttered and blazed! 'Now,' they thought, 'everyone can see that we are the top people here. No one can shine like us – what brilliance! What a light we throw on dark places!'

"And then they were all burnt out."

"That was a lovely tale!" said the queen. "I feel as if I had been in the kitchen all the time, especially with those matches. You shall certainly marry our daughter."

"Yes, yes, of course," said the king. "We'll have the wedding on Monday." And he dropped his royal manner when he spoke, since the young man was now one of the family.

Everything was arranged, and on the eve of the wedding the whole city was lit up. Cakes and buns were thrown to be scrambled for; the street urchins hopped about on tiptoe, cheering and whistling through their fingers. It was a glorious occasion. Just to be there was enough to make anyone happy.

"I suppose I ought to be doing something too," thought the merchant's son. So he bought rockets and whizzbangs, every kind of firework you could think of. Then he put them into his trunk and flew up into the air. Swoosh! Bang! How those fireworks blazed and thundered! All the Turks were leaping into the air with the wonder of it; their slippers were flying about their ears. Never in their lives had they seen such a fantastic show. Now they were certain that the princess was marrying a real Turkish god.

As soon as the merchant's son reached the wood he thought he would go back to the town to hear for himself what the people were saying about his fiery flight. You might have done the same yourself – it was perfectly natural. Goodness, how they were talking! Every person had a different version of the happening, but they all thought it magical.

"I saw the Turkish god himself," said one. "He had eyes like glittering stars, and a beard like the rolling waves!"

"He wore a great cloak of fire," said another. "I saw cherubs peeping from the folds – lovely little things they were."

Oh yes, there was plenty of good listening for the young man. And next day was to be his wedding day.

At last he went back to the wood to get his trunk – but what had become of it? The trunk was burnt to cinders. A spark from the fireworks had set it alight, and all that remained was ashes. He could not fly; so he could not get back to his bride.

All day she stood waiting on the roof. She is waiting still. As for him, he goes wandering round the world, on foot, telling fairy tales. But somehow none is as lighthearted as the one he told of the matches.

TOMKIN AND THE THREE LEGGED STOOL

by

VIVIAN FRENCH

This is a new story by a writer living today; yet it would fit without trouble into any book of traditional folk and fairy tales. Read only a few lines and you will know that the author has a sure foot in that country. For when little Tomkin (living on hard bread and water) dreams of the luxuries he would have if he were king, what are they? Hot cabbage soup and thick red blankets. (This brings to mind an old Russian tale in which a poor peasant tries to imagine the rich life of the Emperor. "He has porridge three times a day!") All the right elements are here: a tailor hero, a tiny kingdom needing a king, a magic

helper. But the arrangement is the author's own. How to reach the cloud? And who but a tailor could deal with the story's problem? That helper, too, is a novelty. A three legged stool? But why not? At least two writers of genius, both in the 19th century, have memorably shown that things, no less than humans and animals, have characters of their own. One was Edward Lear. The other was Andersen. Two examples are in the present book. One further point: this story is so clearly told, so exact in its child-view detail, that listening children must find it an ideal tale to illustrate. Find some paper and start!

There was once a little tailor called Tomkin. He had no mother, no father, no brothers and no sisters. He had nothing that belonged to him except for his needles, his reels of cotton, his scissors, and a three legged stool, but he sang and he whistled as he worked.

One night Tomkin had a dream. He dreamed that instead of eating hard bread and water for his supper he had hot cabbage soup with soft white rolls. He dreamed that instead of sleeping on a cold and draughty bench he had a warm and cosy bed with thick red blankets. He dreamed that instead of sitting all day on a little wooden stool with three legs he sat on a golden throne . . .

Tomkin sat up on his bench and rubbed his eyes.

"Well!" he said. "That was a good dream – the best I've ever had. Hot cabbage soup! Thick red blankets! And me a king – whatever can it mean?" He scratched his head, and looked at his three legged stool.

"What do you think?" he asked.

The three legged stool turned around twice and bowed.

"I think Your Majesty should go out and find your kingdom," it said.

"You're quite right," said Tomkin. "All I do here is mend shirts and stockings and sew on the mayor's buttons twice a week. I'll be off right away." He hopped off the bench and packed a bag with all his needles, three reels of cotton and a pair of sharp scissors.

"Now I'm ready," he said, but he didn't go out through the door.

"What are you waiting for?" asked the three legged stool.

"I was wondering if I'd be lonely, travelling all the way to my kingdom on my own," said Tomkin.

"It might be near, or it might be far," said the three legged stool. "Shall I come with you?"

"Yes, please, " said Tomkin, "and when I'm king I promise I'll make you prime minister."

The stool spun round on one leg and sang:

> *"Promises, promises, one, two, three,*
> *A king will never remember me."*

"Oh, yes, I will," said Tomkin, and they went through the door together.

Tomkin walked along the road with a hop, a skip and a jump, and the three legged stool trundled along beside him. They walked through a forest and over a hill and down into the valley on the other side. Sometimes they talked, and sometimes they were silent, and sometimes

Tomkin whistled a tune and the stool danced on its three wooden legs.

Down in the valley was a wide river and Tomkin and the three legged stool came to a stop.

"Oh, dear," said Tomkin, "I can't swim! Do you think my kingdom is on this side or the other side of the river?"

"It might be far, or it might be near," said the stool. "But as to swimming – just throw me in and hold on tightly!"

Tomkin waded into the rushing water, holding on to the stool. The current caught him and swirled him off his feet, but the wooden stool bobbed and floated on top of the water.

"*Oof!*" spluttered Tomkin, and he kicked and splashed until he and the stool were on the far side of the river. They staggered up the bank, and sat down to rest.

"You're a very good swimmer," Tomkin said to the three legged stool. "And when I'm king I promise I'll make you prime minister."

The stool spun round on two legs and sang.

"Promises, promises, one, two, three,
A king will never remember me."

"Yes, I will," said Tomkin indignantly.

Tomkin and the stool walked on and on, and as they walked they noticed that the grass and bushes on either side of the path were dusty brown. The trees had no leaves and the earth was hard and cracked.

"It looks as if it hasn't rained here for ages and ages," said Tomkin. "But it must be going to rain soon – look at the sky!"

The sky was leaden grey, and a huge black cloud was

swirling round the top of the hill ahead of them. They could see a village half-way up the hill, and beyond the village was a castle.

"Maybe that's my kingdom," Tomkin said.

"Maybe it is," said the stool. "It certainly looks as if all the people have come out to meet us."

Tomkin stopped and stared. The three legged stool was quite right – many men and women and children were hurrying down the hill towards them.

Tomkin shook his head. "I don't think I want to be king here," he said. "All these people look as sad as sad can be."

A bony little girl reached Tomkin and the three legged stool first.

"Oh, please!" she gasped, clutching at Tomkin's arm. "Please – have you come to make it rain?"

"What?" Tomkin said. "What do you mean? There's the biggest blackest cloud I ever saw over there – it must be about to rain puddles and ponds and lakes and seas any moment now."

The little girl began to sob and to cry, although not one tear came out of her eyes.

"But that's just it!" she wailed. "The cloud is always there – but it never, ever rains! All our rivers have dried up, and we've had no water now for days and weeks and months. Our cows and sheep have run away, and we have nothing left to eat but one cupful of flour. All our fields are dry and bare except for one small cabbage. And if it doesn't rain soon, we will all dry up into dust and blow away in the wind."

Tomkin looked around him at all the people. They were gazing at him, their eyes huge and hopeful in their thin pinched faces. He looked up at the black cloud, and he shifted his bag on his back and rubbed his nose.

"Well. . ." he said.

"Ahem," said the three legged stool in a small voice beside him. "Doesn't that cloud look full of rain? As full of rain as a bag might be full of needles and reels of cotton . . . but one snip from your scissors and they'd all fall out!"

"*Oh!*" said Tomkin. "Oh, yes! How clever you are – when I'm king I'm certainly going to make you prime minister!"

The stool spun round on three legs and sang:
"Promises, promises, one, two, three,
A king will never remember me!"

"Just you wait and see!" said Tomkin, and he marched on along the path and up the hill.

"Be careful!" the stool called after him. "A little can go a very long way!"

"I know what I'm doing," said Tomkin.

Up and up he went; past the village and past the castle until he was at the top of the hill and the huge black cloud was billowing just above his head. Tomkin swung the bag off his back and pulled out his scissors.

"Look at me !" he shouted.

Snip! Snap! Rip! Tomkin cut three long slashes right across the cloud. WHOOSH! the rush of rain washed him off his feet and sent him gasping and tumbling all the way back down to the bottom of the hill.

"HURRAH! HURRAH! HURRAH!" shouted the men and the women and the children, and they danced round and round in the silver sheets of pouring rain. They laughed and they sang and they cried and they cheered, and they picked up Tomkin and carried him back up the hill to the castle.

"You must be our king!" they said, and they sat him on a golden throne and put a golden crown on his head. They fetched him hot cabbage soup and soft white rolls, and they showed him his bed heaped with thick red blankets.

At the bottom of the hill the three legged stool stood and waited for Tomkin. It stood there with the rain beating down on it, and a cold wind blowing about it. In a small, sad voice it sang:

"Promises, promises, one, two, three,
When will the king remember me?"

It went on raining. It rained without stopping, day and night, night and day. The trees and the fields grew green, and then became dark and heavy with the never-ending rain. Up in the castle Tomkin laughed and danced and sang, but as the rains went on he watched the rivers begin to flow again, and then fill and fill until they flooded their banks and rushed and gushed all over the countryside. The men and the women and the children stopped being happy and began to complain.

"What's the use of rain if it never stops?" they asked each other. "We were unhappy before, but if the floods wash our village away we'll be even worse off." And they walked up the path to the castle and demanded to see King Tomkin.

"You must stop the rain and bring back the sun," they said. "If you can't, we'll take away your crown and send you off on your travels again."

"Oh, dear," said Tomkin. "Well – maybe I could sew the holes together."

He put his bag on his back and walked out of the castle and up to the top of the hill with the villagers following behind him. The black cloud was still in the sky, but it had poured out so much water that it was now high up, and far beyond his reach. Tomkin rubbed his nose.

"I need a ladder," he said. "I need lots of ladders."

"Then will you make it stop raining?" asked a little boy.

Tomkin nodded. "I'll try," he said.

"Hurrah!" shouted the little boy. "King Tomkin is going to mend the cloud!"

All the men and women and children from the village went hurrying off through the rain to fetch their ladders. They fetched their tables, and they fetched their chairs, and they heaped them one on top of the other into a tower that rose higher and higher.

"It's not high enough," Tomkin said. "What else have you got?"

They brought out beds and baths and chests of drawers. They carried dressers and cupboards and baskets and buckets and boxes, and piled them up and up.

"Is there anything else?" asked Tomkin.

"Nothing," said the villagers, staring at the tottering tower and shaking their dripping heads. "There's not so much as a bead box left to bring."

"All right," said Tomkin. "Now I'll see what I can do." And he began to climb.

Up went Tomkin, pulling himself up the ladders and climbing up and over the cupboards and chairs. Soon he could see the world around him for miles and miles, and still he climbed up and up. The big black cloud grew closer and closer, and he shook the rain from his eyes and kept on climbing.

Tomkin reached the top of the tower. He stood on the highest chair and stretched upwards . . . and he couldn't reach. He could see the three long splits in the cloud, but he was just too far away to touch them.

"I can't do it!" Tomkin said. "I can't reach."

The villagers began to whisper to each other and to mutter and to growl.

"Throw down your crown, Tomkin!" they shouted. "You're no king of ours! Throw down your crown, and be on your way!"

Tomkin looked down. He saw the cold, miserable villagers, and he saw that all their tables and chairs and cupboards and beds and boxes were wet and spoiled. He saw the rain-soaked fields, and the rippling floodwater creeping closer and closer to the village. And far, far off, at the bottom of the path, he saw the three legged stool patiently waiting for him.

Tomkin took a deep breath. "I cut the cloud too deeply and

I've made it rain for ever and ever," he said. "And I forgot my oldest friend. I don't deserve to be a king," and he tossed the crown to the ground. His tears dropped down and mixed with the streams of water flowing down the hill . . . down to the three legged stool.

Up jumped the stool, and hurried up the hill.

"Stop!" it called. "Wait for me!" And it scurried through the groups of wailing villagers to the bottom of the tower. Tomkin was sitting at the top with his head in his hands, but when he heard the stool calling he sat up straight and wiped his eyes.

Everyone watched the stool scrambling up the tower. Up and up it went, and when it reached the top Tomkin held it steady.

"I'm so sorry I forgot you," he said. "I really, truly am."

"No time for that now," said the stool as it balanced itself on top of the very topmost chair. "Come along – climb on me."

Tomkin took his needles and thread out of his bag, and climbed on the stool. He was just high enough to reach the three long rips in the cloud and he began to sew. He sewed all day long without stopping once, and gradually the rain grew less and less, until by the evening there was only a fine mist in the air.

"A couple more stitches and I'll be done," said Tomkin.

"That's good," said the stool.

Tomkin stopped suddenly.

"Oh!" he said. "Oh, no!"

"What's the matter?" asked the stool.

"It's no good," Tomkin said, "it's no good at all. There are needle holes in the cloud at the beginning and end of every stitch. I can see thousands of water drops squeezing through them – I'll *never* be able to stop the rain."

"Nobody wants you to stop the rain for ever," said the stool. "Finish your stitching."

"But it's no good," Tomkin said. "The whole village will be washed away, and it's all my fault." He made his last stitch and pulled it tight.

"Well done," said the stool. "Now look!"

Tomkin looked. The setting sun had come creeping out from behind the cloud and was shining through the mist. A rainbow was shimmering from one side of the hill to the other, and the puddles and ponds and lakes were shining golden mirrors of light.

"KING TOMKIN! KING TOMKIN!" called the villagers. "Come down and take up your crown!"

Tomkin shook his head, and began climbing down the tower with the three legged stool close behind him. Half-way down, a gust of wind blew a flurry of raindrops against Tomkin's face.

"Why!" he said. "The rain's like silver needles! It must be blowing through the needle holes in the cloud – but it isn't rushing and gushing like it was before."

"That's right," said the stool. "But a little can go a very long way."

Tomkin reached the ground, picked up the crown and handed it to the oldest villager.

"I'm not fit to be a king," he said, "but if you want someone wise and clever I think you should ask the three legged stool."

The villager bowed to the stool, and the stool bowed back.

"A king," said the stool, "should always know when he's made a mistake."

"Quite so," said the oldest villager.

"And a king should be willing to work all day without stopping for the good of his people," said the stool.

"My thoughts exactly," said the oldest villager.

"And a king should be as happy when he has nothing but a bag of needles as when he has a golden throne."

"I couldn't have put it better myself," said the oldest villager, and he picked up the golden crown and handed it back to Tomkin.

"Hurrah for King Tomkin!" shouted all the villagers.

Tomkin held up his hand and the men and the women and the children were silent.

"Thank you very much," he said, and he bowed. "But I will only be king if the three legged stool is prime minister."

"It will be my pleasure," said the three legged stool.

"Hurrah for the three legged stool! Three cheers for our prime minister! And three more cheers for our wonderful king!" and the villagers picked Tomkin up and carried him off to the castle.

The three legged stool and the oldest villager walked up the path together.

"The best king of all," said the oldest villager, "is a king who keeps his promises."

And the stool sang:
>   *"Promises, promises, one, two, three,*
>   *This is the king for you and me!"*

and he followed Tomkin into the castle with a hop, a skip and a jump.

HANSEL AND GRETEL

by
THE BROTHERS GRIMM
retold by
NAOMI LEWIS

Not everything in this familiar tale is likeable; for one thing, the mother's (sometimes the stepmother's) nasty behaviour – the witch's too, as well as her horrible end. (For more on witches, see the Introduction.) Yet on the "good" side the tale has features that stir the imagination; once met, they can stay in the mind for life. One is the idea of the white stones that can lead you safely home or back where you wish to be. Another, of course, is the gingerbread house in

*the wood – delightful so long as you don't disturb the witch. Added to
these could be the obliging duck, who takes the children homewards
over the water. Then, to be sure, without the story, would we ever
have had the children's opera Hansel and Gretel, with its memorable
tunes and songs? Its composer, Humperdinck, is not to be confused
with a one-time pop-vocalist who stole the name.*

There was once a woodcutter who lived on the edge of
a great forest with his wife and their two children. The
boy's name was Hansel, the girl's was Gretel. They
were always poor, but now there was famine in the land, and
they had almost nothing to eat.

One night, as the father lay awake, his mind full of worries
and troubles, he said to his wife, "What will become of us all?
How can we feed our poor children?"

"Listen to me, husband," said the wife. "Tomorrow
morning we will take the children into the thickest part of
the forest. We'll light a fire and give them each a piece of
bread, then we'll leave them alone. They'll never find the
way back. And we'll be rid of them."

"No, no, wife," said the man. "We can't do that. I could
never leave my children alone in the forest. They could be
torn to pieces by wild animals."

"What a fool you are!" said the wife. "Do you want all four
of us to die? You might as well start this minute preparing the
wood for our coffins."

On and on she went until he stopped arguing. "All right, all
right," he said. "But I'm very unhappy about your plan."

Now the children, lying awake through hunger, heard this conversation. Gretel began to cry. "All is over with us now," she lamented.

"Hush," said Hansel. "Don't cry. I'll think of a way of saving us."

When the parents had gone to sleep at last, Hansel got up and put on his little coat, and quietly slipped outside. The moon shone so brightly that the white pebbles round the house glittered like newly-minted silver coins. Hansel stooped down and stuffed his pockets with the little stones until they could hold no more. Then he went back to Gretel. "Don't worry," he told her. "Go to sleep. God won't forsake us." And he lay down again.

But not for long. At earliest dawn, before the sun had risen, the woman shook them awake. "Get up, you lazy-bones!" she shouted. "We are going into the forest to fetch wood."

She gave them each a piece of bread, saying, "Now, this is your dinner. Mind you don't eat it too soon, for you'll get no more."

Gretel took charge of the bread, since Hansel's pockets were filled with stones. Then they all started out.

When they had gone a little way, Hansel stopped. He seemed to be looking back. He did this again – then again.

"Hansel, what are you stopping for?" said the father. "You are wasting time. What are you looking at?"

"Oh, father," said Hansel. "I'm just looking at the white cat on the roof. I think he is saying goodbye to me."

"Foolish boy!" said the mother. "That's no cat. It's the sun shining on the chimney."

But Hansel hadn't been looking at the cat. Each time he stopped he had laid down a white pebble.

At last they reached the middle of the forest. "Now, children," said the father, "gather some wood and we'll make a fire."

Hansel and Gretel collected twigs and made a large pile. A fire was lit, and the woman said, "Now, you two, sit by the fire and rest awhile. When we have finished our woodcutting we'll come back and fetch you."

So the two children sat by the blaze and ate their little pieces of bread. They thought that their father was near because they could hear the sound of an axe: *Thud! Thud!* It was no axe, though. The sound came from a branch which the man had tied to a dead tree, so that the wind would blow it backwards and forwards. They sat there waiting for so long that their eyes began to close. Soon they were fast asleep. When they awoke it was dark night. Gretel again began to cry. "How shall we ever get out of the wood?" she asked.

"Don't cry," said Hansel. "Wait until the moon rises; then we'll find our way."

As soon as the full moon rose, Hansel took his sister's hand and began to follow the shining path of pebbles. At daybreak they reached their home.

They knocked at the door, and the mother opened it. Quickly she said, "You bad children, why did you stop so long in the wood? We thought you must be lost." She was angry at their return. The father, though, was delighted. He had never wished to leave them in the wood.

But the family was still desperately poor. One night the children heard their mother say, "All we have left is half a loaf of bread. This time we must take those two even further into the forest, so that they won't find the way back. There is nothing else to be done."

The father shook his head. "We would do better to share our last with the children."

But the wife reminded him that he had given in once. How could he now refuse? "You might as well stop arguing," she declared. What could he do?

The children heard all this, and once again Hansel planned to collect white stones. When the parents slept he crept to the door. But it was locked. Well, another idea came into his mind.

Long before sunrise the mother roused the children for an early start to the forest. Each child was given a tiny piece of bread, to last for the day. Hansel broke up the bread in his pocket – this was his new plan – and carefully dropped a line of crumbs as they walked.

"What are you stopping for?" asked the father. "Why do you keep looking back?"

"Oh, I was looking at the dove on the roof. It seemed to be saying goodbye to me."

"Foolish boy," said the mother. "That's no dove. It's the morning sun shining on the chimney."

Hansel still managed to drop the last of the crumbs. They had by now reached a dense part of the forest, further than they had ever been before. Again a fire was made, and the mother said, "Stay where you are, you two, and if you are tired, go to sleep for a while. When we have finished our work, we will come and collect you."

The children had to share Gretel's bread, since Hansel's had been used to mark the way home. By evening no one had come to fetch them, and at last they fell asleep.

It was quite dark when they woke, but Hansel said, "Don't worry, Gretel. When the moon rises the breadcrumbs will show us the way home."

The moon rose – but where were the crumbs? They had been eaten, every one, by the forest birds.

"We'll find the way," said Hansel. But it was not so easy. Wherever they walked, they still seemed to be in the heart of the wood.

On the third day, hungry and exhausted, they began to despair. But at midday their luck seemed to change. They saw in a tree a lovely snow-white bird. It began to sing, so beautifully that they stopped to listen. Then it fluttered around them and started to fly further into the wood. They followed the bird and saw it alight on the roof of a tiny cottage in a clearing. A strange cottage indeed! The walls were made of bread or cake; the roof was of gingerbread, and the windows were of sparkling sugar.

"This will suit us!" said Hansel. "I'll have a piece of the roof, and you try a window." He reached up and broke off a piece of the gingerbread roof, while Gretel began to taste a corner of window sugar.

But what was this voice calling out from the cottage? It was saying:

"Nibble, nibble, mousekin.
Who's nibbling at my housekin?"

The children looked at each other, then replied:

"Only the wind, nothing more.
The wind is nibbling at your door."

And they boldly went on eating. Hansel took a larger piece of the roof, while Gretel pushed out one of the small round panes of window sugar and sat on the ground to enjoy it.

All at once the door opened and an old, old woman, supporting herself on a crutch, came hobbling out. Hansel and Gretel were so frightened, that they dropped what they held in their hands.

But the old woman only shook her head and said: "Ah, dear children, who brought you here? Come in and stay with me; you will come to no harm."

She took them by the hand and led them into the little house. A nice dinner was set before them, pancakes and sugar, milk, apples, and nuts. After this she showed them two little white beds into which they crept, and felt as if they were in Heaven.

Although the old woman appeared to be so friendly, she was really a wicked old witch who was on the watch for children, and she had built the bread house on purpose to lure them to her. Whenever she could get a child into her clutches she cooked it and ate it, and considered it a grand feast. Witches have red eyes, and can't see very far, but they have keen scent like animals, and can perceive the approach of human beings.

When Hansel and Gretel came near her, she laughed to herself, and said scornfully: "Now I have them, they shan't escape me."

She got up early in the morning, before the children were awake, and when she saw them sleeping, she murmured to herself: "They will be dainty morsels. First the boy."

Seizing Hansel with her bony hand, she carried him off to a little stable, where she shut him up with a barred door; he might shriek as loud as he liked, she took no notice. Then she went to Gretel and shook her till she woke, and cried:

"Get up, little lazy-bones, fetch some water and cook something nice for your brother; he is in the stable, and has to be fattened. When he is nice and fat, I will eat him."

Gretel began to cry bitterly, but it was no use, she had to obey the witch's orders. The best food was now cooked for poor Hansel, but Gretel only had the shells of crayfish.

The old woman hobbled to the stable every morning, and cried: "Hansel, put your finger out for me to feel how fat you are."

Hansel put out a little bone, and the old woman, whose eyes were dim, could not see, and thought it was his finger, and she was much astonished that he did not get fat.

When four weeks had passed, and Hansel still kept thin, she became very impatient and would wait no longer.

"Now then, Gretel," she cried, "bustle along and fetch the water. Fat or thin, tomorrow Hansel will be my dinner."

Oh, how his poor little sister grieved. As she carried the water, the tears streamed down her cheeks.

"Dear God, help us!" she cried. "If only the wild animals in the forest had devoured us, we should, at least, have died together."

"You may spare your lamentations; they will do you no good," said the old woman.

Early in the morning Gretel had to go out to fill the great kettle with water, and then she had to kindle a fire and hang the kettle over it.

"We will bake first," said the old witch. "I have heated the oven and kneaded the dough."

She pushed poor Gretel towards the oven, and said: "Creep in and see if it is properly heated, and then we will put the bread in."

She meant, when Gretel had got in, to shut the door and roast her.

But Gretel saw her intention, and said: "I don't know how to get in. How am I to manage it?"

"Stupid girl!" cried the witch. "The opening is big enough; you can see that I could get into it myself."

She hobbled up, and stuck her head into the oven. But Gretel gave her a push which sent the witch right in, and then she banged the door and bolted it.

And that was the end of the witch.

Then Gretel ran as fast as she could to the stable, opened the door, and cried out, "Hansel, we are saved. The old witch is dead."

Hansel sprang out, like a bird from a cage when the door is set open. How delighted they were. They fell upon each other's necks, and kissed each other, and danced about for joy.

As they had nothing more to fear, they went into the witch's house, and they found chests in every corner full of pearls and precious stones.

"These are better than pebbles," said Hansel, as he filled his pockets.

Gretel said, "I must take some home with me too." And she filled her apron.

"Now we must go," said Hansel. "We have to find a way out of the magic power of this wood."

Before they had gone very far, they came to a great piece of water.

"We can't get across it," said Hansel. "I see no stepping-stones and no bridge."

"And there are no boats either," answered Gretel. "But there is a duck swimming, it will help us over if we ask it."

So she cried:

> *"Here, a needy pair, we stand,*
> *No bridge or boat is near at hand.*
> *Gentle duck, that cries Quack, Quack,*
> *Will you take us on your back?"*

The duck came swimming towards them, and Hansel got on its back, and told his sister to sit on his knee.

"No," answered Gretel, "it will be too heavy for the duck; it must take us over one after the other."

The good creature did this, and when they had got safely

over and walked for a while, the wood seemed to grow more and more familiar to them, and at last they saw their father's cottage in the distance. They began to run, and rushed inside, where they threw their arms around their father's neck. The man had not had a single happy moment since he had deserted his children in the wood, and in the meantime his wife had died.

Gretel shook her apron and scattered the pearls and precious stones all over the floor, and Hansel added handful after handful out of his pockets.

So all their troubles came to an end, and they lived together happily ever after.

THE GOBLIN
AT THE
GROCER'S

by
HANS CHRISTIAN
ANDERSEN

translated by
NAOMI LEWIS

This brilliant little story could have come from no other hand than Andersen's. First published in 1853, a vintage period, (the 65th tale in his total of 156) it's an admired favourite of Andersen devotees; yet it is still not as widely known as it should be. Well, here it is, witty, amusing, cheerful even. "Why am I smiling?" you may suddenly ask yourself as you read. This applies not only to the joyfully ludicrous night-time interlude. But running through the whole is a question, a problem of choice, and that's a matter that can touch most of us, one way or another. What cunning then to make the problem clear through an imp or fairy character. Our goblin-hero (pixie, as some translators prefer) is a nisse, a Danish house spirit. But, simple as he may seem, and so direct in his likings, he thinks.

And here is something for sleuths. In most of his shorter tales of the wholly invented kind, Andersen himself makes a short appearance, as a student perhaps, a lodger, a storyteller (or listener), a maker of paper dolls (one of his skills). Maybe he was the child who spoke the truth about the Emperor's unseen clothes. In the story here you can see him of course as the penniless student poet. But still more, he is the goblin, a much more sly and observant view of himself. Note how the creature can perceive, through the keyhole, hour after hour, marvels invisible to the worthy grocer below. Yet the grocer is to be valued for other reasons. Which to choose? It has to be said that Andersen (but through his genius) did at last achieve both.

There was once a student, a proper student; he lived in an attic and owned nothing at all. There was also a grocer, a proper grocer; he lived on the ground floor and owned the whole house. And so it was with the grocer that the goblin chose to make his home. Besides, every Christmas he was given a bowl of porridge with a great lump of butter in it. The grocer could manage that easily, and so the goblin stayed in the shop. There's a moral there somewhere, if you look for it.

One evening the student came in through the back door to buy some candles and cheese. His shopping was quickly done and paid for, and the grocer and his wife nodded "Good evening". The wife could do more than nod, though; she was a chatterbox – talk, talk, talk. She had what they call the gift of the gab, no doubt about that. The student nodded back – and then his eye fell on something written on the paper wrapping the cheese, and he stood there reading it. It was a page torn from an old book, one which should never have been torn up at all, an old book full of poetry.

"There's more of that book if you want it," said the grocer. "I gave an old woman some coffee beans for it. You can have the rest for sixpence if you like."

"Thank you," said the student. "Let me have it instead of the cheese. I can do very well with bread. It's a shame to use such a book for wrapping paper! You are an excellent man, a practical man – but you have no more idea of poetry than that tub over there."

Now this was a rude thing to say, especially the part about the tub; but the grocer laughed, and the student laughed; after all, it was only a kind of joke. But the little goblin was annoyed that anyone should dare to speak like that to the grocer – his landlord too – an important person who owned the whole house and sold the best quality butter.

That night, when the shop was shut and everyone but the student had gone to bed, the goblin tiptoed in and borrowed the grocer's wife's gift of the gab, for she had no need of it while she was asleep. Then, whatever object he put it on in the room was able to voice its views and opinions quite as well as the lady herself. But only one thing at a time could have it, and that was a blessing; otherwise they would all have been chattering away at once.

First, the goblin placed the gift of the gab on the tub where the old newspapers were kept. "Is it really true," he asked, "that you don't know what poetry is?"

"Of course I know!" said the tub. "It's something you find

at the bottom of the page in a newspaper; people cut it out. I rather think that I have more poetry in me than the student has – yet I'm only a humble tub compared with the grocer."

Then the goblin placed the gift of the gab on the coffee mill. Goodness, how it clattered on! After that he put it on the butter-cask, then the cash-till. They all echoed the views of the tub, and the views of the majority have to be respected.

"Now I can put that student in his place," said the goblin, and he tiptoed softly up the back staircase to the attic where the student lived. There was a light inside, and the goblin peeped through the keyhole and saw the young man reading the tattered book from the shop.

But how bright it was in the room! Out of the book rose a shining beam of light; it became a tree-stem, the trunk of a noble tree that soared up and spread its branches over the student. The leaves were fresh and green, and every flower was the face of a lovely girl; some had dark mysterious eyes, some had eyes of sparkling blue. Every fruit was a shining star, and the air was filled with an indescribably beautiful sound of singing.

The little goblin had never seen or known of such wonders; he could never have imagined them, even. And so he stayed at the door, standing on tiptoe, peeping in, gazing and gazing, until the light in the room went out. The student must have blown out his candle and gone to bed – but still the goblin could not tear himself away; his head rang with the marvellous music, which still echoed in the air, lulling the student to sleep.

"This is beyond belief," said the goblin to himself. "I certainly never expected anything of the kind. I think I shall stay in the attic with the student." And then he pondered a while, and then he sighed. "One must be sensible," he said. "The student hasn't any porridge."

And so – yes – he went down again to the grocer's shop. It was a good thing he did, because the tub had nearly worn out the gift of the gab, what with telling everyone all the news and views of the papers stacked inside. It had done so from one angle, and was just about to turn over and gabble it all again from another, when the goblin took the gab back to the sleeping wife. And from that time the whole shop, from the cash-till to the firewood, took all their opinions from the tub; they held it in such respect that, ever after, when the grocer was reading out criticisms of plays or books from the newspapers, they thought that he had learnt it all from the tub.

But the goblin could no longer sit quietly listening to all the wisdom and good sense that was uttered down in the shop. No – the moment the light began to shine through the attic door, he seemed to be drawn there by powerful strings, and up he had to go and station himself at the keyhole. And each time that he did this, a sense of unutterable grandeur would sweep through him – the kind of feeling that we might have at the sight of a stormy sea whose waves are so wild that God himself might be riding over them in the blast. How wonderful it would be to sit under the tree with the student! But that could never be.

Meanwhile, he was grateful to have the keyhole. He gazed

through it every night, standing there on the bleak landing even when the autumn winds blew through the skylight, making him nearly freeze with cold. Yet he felt nothing of this until the light went out in the attic room and the music faded away in the howling of the wind. Brrr! Then he would realize how cold he was, and would creep down again to his secret corner of the shop where it was so snug and warm. Soon there would be the Christmas bowl of porridge with its great lump of butter. Yes – the grocer was the one to choose after all.

But late one night the goblin was woken up by a frightful commotion. People were banging at the shutters; the watchman was blowing his whistle; a fire had broken out, and the whole street seemed ablaze. Which house was burning? This one or the next? Where *was* the fire? What screams! What panic! What a fuss! The grocer's wife was so flustered that she took her gold earrings from her ears and put them in her pocket, so that she might at least save *some*thing. The grocer dashed after his bonds, the maid after the silk shawl that she had bought with her wages. Everyone ran to collect the thing he or she prized most highly.

And the little goblin did so too. In a bound or two he was up the stairs and in the room of the student, who was standing quite calmly at the open window, looking out at the fire in the house across the road. The goblin seized the wonderful book from the table, put it in his scarlet cap, and hugged it with both arms. The most precious thing in the house was saved! Then he rushed up to the roof, right to the top of the chimney stack, and there he sat, lit up by the flames of the house on fire over the way, still firmly clasping the red cap with the treasure inside.

Now he knew where his heart lay; student? – grocer? – his choice was clear.

But when the fire had been put out, and the goblin had had time to think more calmly – well . . .

"I'll divide my time between them," he decided. "I can't quite give up the grocer, because of the porridge."

Just like a human, really. We too like to keep on good terms with the grocer, because of the porridge.

THE TWELVE DANCING PRINCESSES

by

THE BROTHERS GRIMM

translated by

STEPHEN CORRIN

One aspect of this attractive tale from the Grimms should have particular appeal to the slightly older young today: those spirited royal daughters – how do they outwit their father king, and dance their shoes to pieces every night? Sadly, real life, even in palaces, has other laws. The many oppressed daughters of England's George III must have sighed with longing had they known this tale. Even so, the fairy tale girls cannot win. An old (or redundant) soldier solves the problem, and he is the true main lead. Nor is this the only tale in which he (or another of his kind) has the hero's role. The frequent European wars – look where you like in history

– left numbers of these penniless wanderers on the roads. At least in story they could gain the highest prize. Easily too: a cloak of invisibility, a shrewd word of advice (both freely provided by a passing old woman) – what more do you need?

The shoes themselves have an interest. They are significant enough to provide the title for various folk and fairy tales known to the Grimms, versions perhaps of the present story. Andersen himself wrote a some-what sinister tale of shoes with a dancing power of their own. There's a British instance too. In the Orkneys tale "Kate Crackernuts" (see Joseph Jacob's English Fairy Tales*), a prince is wasting away through being nightly lured to dance with fairies under the hill.*

But it need not be the plot that stays, unasked, in the mind. If it turns out to be the midnight lake, the forest of silver and golden leaves, the dream-like thrill of the dance itself, or all of these, they are not the least offerings of this fairy tale. Hold on to them!

There was once a king who had twelve daughters, each one more beautiful than the next. They slept together in one room where their beds stood in a row, and in the evening, when they lay down, the king locked the door and bolted it. But when he unlocked the door next morning he saw that their shoes were worn right through with dancing, and nobody could think how that had come about. Then the king issued a proclamation that whoever could find out where they had danced in the night could choose one of them as his wife and become king after his death. But if anyone presented him-self and had not solved the mystery after three days and nights, then he should forfeit his life.

In due course a king's son presented himself and volun-teered to take the risk. He was given a warm welcome, and in the evening he was taken to a room adjoining the bedroom of the princesses. A bed was set up for him there, and he was to keep watch to see where they went and where they danced. And in order that they shouldn't do anything in secret or leave their room, the doors between the rooms were left open. But after a while the eyes of the king's son began to feel as heavy as lead, and he dozed off. And when he awoke in the morning, he saw that all twelve had been dancing, for there were their shoes with holes in the soles. It was no different on the second and third night, and so the king's son was beheaded without mercy. After this many more suitors came forward to risk their lives in this daring adventure, but there wasn't one that did not end up dead.

Now it so happened that a poor soldier, who had been wounded in battle and was no longer fit for service, found himself on the road to the city where the king dwelt. He chanced to meet an old woman, who asked him where he was bound for.

"I don't quite know the answer to that myself," he replied, and then, half-jokingly, he added, "I'd like to find out where the king's daughters dance their shoes out. Then, one day, who knows, I might wear the king's crown."

"Well, it's not as hard as all that," said the old woman. "You must avoid drinking the wine the princesses will bring you in the evening, and then pretend you're sound asleep." Whereupon she gave him a little cloak, saying, "When you wrap this around yourself you'll be invisible and then you'll be able to follow the twelve princesses."

With the benefit of this good advice, the soldier took his

courage in both hands and presented himself before the king as a suitor.

He was well received, like all the others, and was given princely garments to put on. In the evening, when it was time to go to bed, he was led to the adjoining room, and the eldest of the princesses brought him a cup of wine. But the soldier had tied a sponge under his chin; he allowed the wine to run into the sponge and did not drink a single drop. Then he lay down and after a while began to snore as though he were sleeping like a log. The king's twelve daughters heard him snore and laughed. The eldest sister said, "There goes another who has thrown away his life." Then they got up, opened cupboards, chests and cases, and brought out some splendid dresses. They smartened themselves up in front of mirrors, and jumped about the room, looking forward to the dance. Only the youngest said, "I don't know why you're all making so merry; I've got this odd feeling that there's some bad luck coming our way."

"You're a silly goose," said the eldest, "you're always fearful something bad is going to happen. Have you forgotten how many princes have already watched us in vain? Even if I hadn't bothered to give the soldier the sleeping potion, the silly oaf would still be dead asleep." When they were ready, they had another look at the soldier, but his eyes were closed tight, and he didn't stir a muscle, and so they thought they were perfectly safe. Then the eldest went to her bed and struck it hard; straight away it sank into the ground, and they all followed it down through the opening, one after the other, the eldest in front. The soldier, who had watched everything, didn't waste any time, wrapped his cloak around him and went down after the youngest princess. But about half-way down, on the steps, he trod on her gown. She was frightened and cried out, "What's that! Who's pulling on my dress?"

"Don't be so silly!" said the eldest. "You must have caught it on a hook."

So they continued down all the steps, and when they were at the bottom, they were in a wonderful avenue of trees where all the leaves were of silver, gleaming and glittering. The soldier thought to himself, "I'd better get some evidence of this to take back with me," and so he broke off one of the branches. There followed a mighty cracking noise from the tree and the youngest princess cried out again, "Something's wrong! Didn't you hear that noise?" The eldest princess replied, "Those are salvoes of joy because we have set our princes free once again."

Then they came to an avenue of trees where all the leaves were of gold and finally to a third avenue where they were shining diamonds. The soldier tore off a bunch from both of these, and each time there was a crack so that the youngest princess collapsed from fright. But the eldest sister insisted that the sounds were only salvoes of rejoicing.

They went on further until they came to a great stretch of water on which were twelve little boats, and in each boat sat a handsome prince. They had been expecting the princesses, and each prince took a sister into his boat, but the soldier got in with the youngest. Then the prince said, "I don't understand, the boat is much heavier today. I have to row with all my strength if I'm to keep moving."

"It must be the warm weather," said the princess. "I'm feeling very hot myself."

Now on the other side of the water stood a beautiful, brightly illuminated castle from which came joyous resounding music of drums and trumpets. They rowed across to it, went in, and each prince danced with his chosen princess. The soldier, however, quite invisible, danced alone, and when one of the princesses took a cup of wine he drank it up so that it was empty when she put it to her lips. The youngest was quite upset by this but her eldest sister always contrived to calm her.

And so they went on dancing till three o'clock in the morning, and by then all their slippers had been danced right through and the dancing had to stop.

The princes took them back across the water in the boats, but this time the soldier sat in front, next to the eldest princess. When they reached the bank they said farewell to the princes and promised they would come again the next night. When they reached the stairs, the soldier ran on ahead and got into his bed, and when the twelve princesses climbed, slow and weary, up the steps, he was already snoring so loudly that they could all hear him, and they told one another, "We're safe from that one." Then they took off their beautiful dresses, put them away, placed their danced-out shoes under the bed and went to sleep.

The next morning the soldier didn't wish to say anything; he only wanted to see the wonderful things happening again, and so he went with the twelve princesses on the second and third nights. It all happened again, just as it had on the first night – the princesses danced their slippers right through just as before.

On the third visit, however, he took the drinking cup as a proof.

When the time came for him to make his answer before the king, he tucked away the three branches and the cup and stood before him, while the twelve sisters stood hidden behind the door and listened to what he would say.

When the king put the question, "Where have my twelve daughters been dancing their shoes out in the night?" the soldier replied, "With twelve princes in an underground castle," and he went on to relate how it had all taken place, and displayed the branches and the cup as proof.

The king then sent for his daughters and asked them if what the soldier had reported was true, and since they could see that they had been discovered and that telling lies would be no use, they had to admit everything. Then the king asked the soldier which one he would take as his wife and he replied, "I'm not so young any more, so I'll take the eldest." And so, on that very same day, the wedding was celebrated and the kingdom was promised to him after the king's death.

As for the princes, however, they remained spellbound underground for as many more days as the number of nights they had danced with the twelve princesses.

THE WILD SWANS

by

HANS CHRISTIAN ANDERSEN

translated by

NAOMI LEWIS

An early work – it was written in 1837 – this is Andersen's own version of a traditional fairy tale. (You may well know the plot.) It was probably the last of his tales to be based on anything but his own invention. Indeed, he had already discovered his unique gift. The little 1837 booklet that contained this story, also held one of his most enduring and superb invented tales, "The Steadfast Tin Soldier." But even in "The Wild Swans", Andersen's voice sounds clearly in the telling, most of all in the descriptive scenes: the woodland lit with summer, the churchyard with the lamias, "those witches that are half snake, half woman". But what in particular must have led him to this story was the great flight through the sky, with its marvellous cloud scenes, so real, yet so soon

dissolving, where "sea and air are ever in motion, ever changing; no vision ever comes to the watcher twice."

Does the plight of the youngest brother, left with one swan-wing, trouble you? It disturbed a recent writer, Ursula Synge: her novel Swan's Wing *wonderfully tells of his journey, with covering cloak, in desperate search of wholeness. It is well worth discovering.*

Far, far away, in the land where the swallows fly during our winter, there lived a king who had eleven sons and one daughter, Elisa. The eleven brothers – princes all of them – went to school, each wearing a star at his heart and a sword at his side. They wrote on leaves of gold with diamond pencils; whatever they read, they learnt at once. You could tell straight off that they were princes! Their sister Elisa sat on a little stool made of looking-glass, and had a picture book that cost half a kingdom.

Oh, they lived royally, those children! But it did not last. The King, their father, married an evil queen, and she didn't care for the children at all. They realised this on the very first day. A great celebration was held to welcome her, and the children, too, decided to play at guests-for-tea. But instead of the cakes and roasted apples which they were usually given, the queen allowed them only a cupful of sand. They would have to pretend that it was cakes and apples, she told them.

A week later, she sent off little Elisa into the country, to live with a peasant family. And it wasn't long before she had filled the king's head with such shocking tales about the poor young princes that he wished to have nothing more to do with them.

"Out you go!" said the wicked queen to the boys. "Fend for yourselves as you may. Fly off as voiceless birds!"

Yet she could not do as much harm as she wished, for they turned into eleven beautiful wild swans. With a strange cry, they flew out of the palace windows, over the fields and forests, far away.

Early in the morning when they passed the place where their sister Elisa had been sent, they circled about the cottage roof, flapping their wings and craning their necks. But nobody heard or saw. At last they had to fly on, upwards into the clouds, out into the wide world.

Poor little Elisa sat in the cottage playing with a green leaf, the only toy she had. She pricked a hole in it and peeped through at the sun. The brightness seemed like the bright eyes of her brothers.

Time passed, one day just like another. But whenever the wind blew through the garden, it whispered to the roses: "Who could be more beautiful than you?"

And the roses would answer, "Elisa is more beautiful."

What they said was the truth.

When Elisa was fifteen she was brought back to the palace. The evil queen, seeing how beautiful she was, was very vexed indeed. She would have promptly turned her into another wild swan like her brothers, but she did not dare just yet, for the king had asked to see his daughter.

Early next morning, the queen went into the bathroom with three toads. She kissed the first and said, "Hop onto Elisa's head, and make her as slow and dull as you." Kissing the second, she said, "Make her look just like you, so that her father will not know her." Then she kissed the third toad, whispering, "Fill her with evil, so that she knows no peace." She put the toads into the clear water, which at once took on a strange greenish tinge. Yet Elisa seemed not to notice them. And when she rose from the water, they were gone; but three scarlet poppies were floating there. If the toads had not been poisoned by the kiss of the wicked queen, they would have become red roses. But flowers they had become from Elisa's touch alone.

When the queen perceived how she had failed, she rubbed Elisa's skin with dark brown walnut juice and made her hair look wild and tangled. You wouldn't have recognized her!

And so, when her father saw her, he was shocked.

"That is not my daughter!" he declared.

No one else at court would have anything to do with her except the watchdog and the swallows and who ever bothered about what *they* thought?

Poor Elisa started to cry. She crept out of the palace, and walked all day through field and moor and meadow, until she reached a great dark forest, leading to the sea. She had no idea where she was but she fixed her mind on her brothers. They had been driven forth like herself, and now she would go to the ends of the earth to find them.

Night fell, and she lay down on the moss. All was silent; the air was mild and touched with a greenish light – it came from hundreds of glow-worms. There were so many that when she gently touched a branch, a shower of the shining creatures dropped down like stars.

All that night she dreamt about her brothers. They were playing together, as they did when they were children, writing with the diamond pencils on the leaves of gold, looking at the beautiful picture book that had cost half a kingdom. Only now they were setting down all that had befallen them, bold deeds and strange adventures. Everything in the picture book seemed to come alive; the birds sang, the people stepped out of the pages and spoke to her. But when she turned over a page they jumped straight back, so as not to get into the wrong picture.

When she awoke the sun was high overhead, though she could hardly see through the thick leaves and branches of the trees. But where the sunbeams shimmered through the moving leaves there was a dancing golden haze. The air was filled with the smell of fresh green grass; the birds flew so near that they seemed about to perch on her shoulder. She heard the splashing of water; it came from a spring which flowed into a pool, so clear that you could see the sandy bed below.

But when Elisa saw her own face in the water, she was startled – it was so grimy and strange. She dipped her hand into the pool and rubbed her eyes and forehead – what a contrast! Her own clear skin shone through. She took off her clothes and stepped into the fresh cool water – and a more beautiful princess could not have been found anywhere in the world.

As she set off again, she met an old woman, who gave her some berries from a basket that she was carrying. Elisa asked her if she had come across eleven princes riding through the forest.

"No," said the old woman. "But yesterday I saw eleven swans with golden crowns on their heads swimming down yonder river." Elisa thanked her and walked along the winding water until it reached the sea. There the great ocean lay before her. What was she to do?

Then she saw, scattered about the seagrass, eleven swan's feathers. She looked up; eleven wild swans were flying towards the land, like a long white ribbon. Each had a golden crown on its head. Flapping their great wings, they landed near her.

A moment later the sun sank below the water; the swans seemed to shed their feathery covering – and there stood eleven handsome princes. Elisa ran forward and threw herself into their arms, calling them each by name. They in turn were overjoyed to see their little sister, and they told her their strange tale.

"We brothers," said the oldest, "have to fly as swans so long as the sun is in the sky. When night has come we return to human shape; that is why we must look for a landing place well before sunset. If we were flying high in the air when darkness came, we should hurtle down as humans to our deaths.

"We do not dwell here any more. Our home is now a land far across the sea. To reach it we have to cross the vast ocean

– and there is no island where we can rest in our human form during the night. Only one thing saves us. About half-way across, a little rock rises out of the water – just large enough to hold us standing close together. If it were not there, we would never be able to visit our native land again, since we need the two longest days of the year for our flight. Once a year we fly over this mighty forest, and gaze at the palace where we were born, and circle over the tower of the church where our mother is buried.

"The wild horses gallop across the plains as they did in our childhood; the charcoal-burner still sings the old songs that we danced to as children. Here is our native ground, the place that will always draw us back.

"But tomorrow we must set off again for that other land, and we cannot return for another year. Have you the courage to come with us, little sister?"

"Oh, take me with you," Elisa said.

All that night they set about weaving a net of willow bark and rushes. When the sun rose and the brothers turned into swans, they picked up the net with their beaks, and flew with Elisa into the clouds. One hovered just overhead to shade her from the sun's hot rays.

Now they had reached such a height that the first ship they saw looked like a white seagull resting on the water. A great cloud lay behind them, a mountain of cloud, and on it Elisa saw the shadows of herself and her brothers. They were like giants' shadows, vast and wonderful. But the sun rose higher and cloud and shadow pictures disappeared.

All the long day they flew, like arrows in the sky. Yet, swift as they were, they were slower than at other times, for they now had their sister to carry. Night was near, the air was full of thunder, but there was still no sign of the tiny rock. Elisa looked down with terror. At any moment now her brothers would change to humans and all would fall to their deaths.

Black clouds surrounded them; storm winds churned the leaden water; flash after flash of lightning pierced the gloom.

Suddenly, the birds headed downwards. The sun was already half-way into the sea – but now, for the first time, she saw the little rock; it could have been a seal's head looking out of the water. Then her feet touched the ground, and at that moment the sun went out like the last spark on a piece of burning paper. All round her stood her brothers, human now, sheltering her from the dashing waves.

At dawn the air was clear and still. The sun rose; the eleven swans soared from the rock, with Elisa on her airy raft, and went on with their journey. From far above, the white foam on the dark green waves looked like thousands of floating swans.

Then Elisa looked ahead, and beheld a range of mountains, with glittering icy peaks, in their midst was a mighty palace, at least a mile in length. Below were groves of waving palm trees; and wonderful flowers, vast in size, like mill-wheels. Yet all this seemed suspended in the air. Was it the land they were making for? But the swans shook their heads. What she was seeing, they told her, was the cloud palace of the fairy Morgana, lovely but ever-changing; no mortal might enter there.

And as Elisa gazed, mountains, palace, trees and flowers all dissolved, and in their place rose a score of noble churches, with lofty towers. She thought that she heard organ music – or was it the sound of the sea? Then, when they seemed quite near, the churches changed to a fleet of ships sailing just below. She looked again – there were no ships; all she saw was a whirl of mist over the water. Sea and air and sky are ever in motion, ever changing; no vision comes to the watcher twice.

And then Elisa glimpsed land at last. Blue mountains of rare beauty rose up before her; she could just discern forests of cedar, cities and palaces. The swans came down, and Elisa found herself at the mouth of a hillside cave; an opening almost hidden by a web of vines and other delicate greenery.

"You can sleep here safely," the youngest brother said.

Was it a dream? She thought that she was flying through the air, straight to the cloud-castle of the fairy Morgana. The fairy herself came to meet her. She was radiant and beautiful – but she was also very much like the old woman who had given her berries in the forest, and had told her of the swans with golden crowns.

"Your brothers *can* be freed," said the fairy. "But it will take no ordinary courage. Look at this stinging nettle. It grows plentifully round the cave where you are now sleeping

– and in only one other place: on churchyard graves. Now, first you must gather them yourself, though they will sting and burn your skin. Then you must tread on them with bare feet until they are like flax. This you must twist into thread and weave into cloth; from it you must make eleven shirts like coats of mail with sleeves. Throw one of these over each of your brothers and the spell will break. But – this is important – until you finish your task, even if it takes years, you must not speak. A single word will pierce your brothers' hearts like a knife. Their lives depend on your silence. Remember!"

She touched Elisa's hand with the nettle. It scorched her skin like fire, and she awoke. It was bright daylight; nearby lay a nettle like the one she had seen in her dream. Elisa went outside the cave – yes, there the nettles were! She would start at once. She plucked an armful, trampled them with bare feet, and began to twist the green flax into thread.

At sunset her brothers returned. At first her silence alarmed them. But then they guessed that she must be doing this strange work for their sakes.

All that night she worked. When day returned, the swan-brothers flew far afield, and she sat alone, but never did time go so fast. One shirt was already finished, and she started on the next.

All at once, a sound rang through the mountains – the sound of a distant hunting horn. She heard the barking of dogs and she was seized with terror.

Then a great hound sprang out of the bushes. It was followed at once by another, then another; they made for the mouth of the cave. Before many minutes, all the huntsmen had gathered at her hiding place, and the most handsome of all stepped forward. He was the king of that land. He saw Elisa, and she seemed to him the most beautiful girl in the world.

"How do you come to be here?" he asked.

Elisa shook her head; she dared not speak.

"Come with me," said the king. "If you are as good as you are beautiful, you shall wear a gold crown on your head, and the finest of my castles shall be your home."

He lifted her onto his horse and they galloped off through the mountains. His companions rode behind.

They reached the royal city at day's end. The king led Elisa into his palace, where sparkling fountains splashed into marble pools and the lofty walls and ceilings were covered with marvellous paintings. But she wept and grieved and saw nothing. Listless and pale, she let the women dress her in royal robes, twine her hair with pearls and cover her damaged hands with gloves.

And so at last she entered the great hall. She was so dazzlingly beautiful that all the court bowed low before her and the king announced that she would be his bride. But the archbishop shook his head and whispered that the wood maiden from the forest must surely be a sorceress who had cast a spell on his heart.

Yet the king would not hear a word against her. He ordered the music to strike up and the rarest dishes to be served; she was taken through fragrant gardens and splendid halls. But nothing touched her grief. Then the king showed her a little room which would be her own. Carpeted in green, hung with costly green tapestries, it was made to look like the cave where she had been found. On the floor lay the bundle of nettles and flax; from the ceiling hung the one shirt that she had finished. A huntsman had brought these things along as a curiosity.

"Here you can dream yourself back in your old home," said the king. "Now when you wish, you can amuse yourself by thinking of that bygone time."

When Elisa saw what was so near to her heart, a smile came to her lips, colour returned to her face and she kissed the king's hand. He took her in his arms and gave commands for all the church bells to be rung for their wedding. The lovely mute girl from the forest would be queen.

Then came the wedding day. The archbishop himself had to place the crown on Elisa's head, and he pressed it down so spitefully that it hurt. But she felt a deep affection for the good and handsome king and day by day, she loved him more and more. If only she could speak! But first, she had to complete her task. So each night, as the king slept, she would steal from his side, and go to her work in the room like a green cave. Six shirts were now complete. But she had no more flax. And only in the churchyard could she find the right nettles.

So at midnight, full of fear, she crept down through the moonlit garden, along the great avenues, and out into the lonely streets that led to the churchyard. What a sight met her eyes! A ring of lamias, those witches that are half snake, half woman, sat round the largest gravestone. Elisa had to pass close by them, and they fastened their dreadful gaze upon her; but she prayed for safety, gathered the nettles and carried them back to the palace.

But not unnoticed. One person had seen and followed her; the archbishop. So his suspicions were true! The new queen *was* a witch.

In the church, after the service, he told all this to the king. The carved saints shook their heads as if to say – "It is not so! Elisa is innocent!" But the archbishop chose to take this differently; the saints were bearing witness against her. They were shaking their heads at her sins.

Two heavy tears rolled down the king's face, and he went home with a troubled heart. He pretended to sleep at night, but no sleep came. Now, day by day, he grew more wretched. This troubled Elisa sorely, and added to her grief about her brothers. Her tears ran down on her royal velvet and purple and lay there like diamonds; but people saw only her beauty and her rich attire and wished that *they* were queen.

Still, her task was nearly done, for only a single shirt remained to be made. The trouble was that again she had no more flax, not a single nettle.

Once more she would have to go to the churchyard. She thought fearfully of the lonely midnight journey; but then she thought of her brothers.

She went – and the king and the archbishop followed her. They saw her disappear through the iron gates of the churchyard; they saw the frightful lamias on the graves. The king turned away in grief, for he thought that she had come to seek the company of these monsters – his own Elisa, his queen.

"The people shall judge her!" he said. And this the people did. They proclaimed her guilty, and ordered her to be burnt at the stake.

She was taken from the splendour of the palace and thrust into a dungeon, damp and dark. Instead of silken sheets and velvet pillows, the nettles and nettle-work cloth from her room had been tossed in. But she could have asked for no better gift. While boys outside sang jeering songs – "The witch! The witch!" – she began to work on the last of the shirts.

The archbishop had arranged to spend the final hours in prayer with her; but when he came, Elisa shook her head and pointed to the door. Her work must be finished that night. The archbishop went away, muttering angry words.

Poor Elisa! If only she could speak. Little mice ran over the floor; they dragged the nettles towards her, doing all that they could to help. A thrush sang all night through at the bars to give her hope.

At first light, an hour before sunrise, the eleven brothers, in human form, stood at the castle gate and demanded to see the king. Impossible! was the answer. The king was asleep and could not be disturbed. They begged and pleaded; they threatened; the guard came down to see what the noise was about. At last it brought down the king himself.

At that very moment the sun rose. Where were the eleven young men? Nowhere. But over the palace flew eleven wild swans.

From earliest daylight, crowds of people had jostled through the city gates; they all wanted to see the burning of the witch. There she was, in a cart dragged along by a forlorn old horse. She was wearing a smock made from coarse sacking; her lovely hair hung loose about her face; her cheeks were deathly pale, but her fingers never stopped working at the last of the green nettle shirts. The other ten lay at her feet. The crowds mocked and yelled:

"Look at the witch! See what she's up to! Still at her filthy witchcraft! Get it away from her! Tear it into a thousand pieces!"

They surged forward, and were just about to destroy her precious handiwork when down flew eleven great white swans. Beating their wings, they settled on the cart. The mob drew back in fear.

"It's a sign from heaven," some of them whispered.

"She must be innocent."

The executioner seized her hand – but she quickly flung the eleven garments over the swans. In their place were eleven handsome princes. Only the youngest had a swan's wing instead of an arm, because Elisa had not time to finish the last sleeve.

"Now I may speak," she said. "I am no witch. I am innocent."

The people hung their heads and kneeled before her.

"Yes, indeed she is innocent," said the eldest brother. And he began to tell their long, strange story. As he spoke, a fragrance as from millions of roses filled the air; every piece of wood in the stake had taken root and put forth branches. There stood a mighty bush of the loveliest red roses. High at the summit was a single white flower, shining like a star. The king reached up and plucked it and laid it on Elisa's heart.

Then all the church bells rang of their own accord, and great flocks of birds flew overhead. And so began the journey back to the palace. A more joyful and more marvellous procession no king has ever yet seen.

THE FAIRY GOD-DAUGHTER

by
JEAN MORRIS

This enjoyable story does not aim to be an imitation fairy tale of the traditional kind. It focuses on a significant and formidable character, yet one who rarely appears, and never in lead place; each time, her errand over, she returns to her own affairs. Who? The fairy godmother. And what are her affairs? The answer – or one of them – is in this story. But the theme that it really explores, in its entertaining detail, is the use of magic – its powers and its limits. The short-cut of illusion: wonderful – but are there possibly flaws? It's not a trivial subject: computers and calculators – aren't they a form of short-cut illusion?

For a full-length study of magic in the human world, no better book in story form exists than Ursula Le Guin's A Wizard of Earthsea, *one of the essential magical novels of the century. Jean Morris herself has written at least two remarkable novels: read them, though you may have to track them through a library; you won't forget them. One – the main one – is* The Donkey's Crusade *(1983). The other is* The Troy Game *(1987). Older teenagers should try* The Paper Canoe. *Morris's light touch and fund of unpredictable knowledge can already be seen in the short story here. In her full-length books her use of language is so sparing, so reasoned and practical, so basic to life, that it seems natural rather than supernatural. Could she have learnt this from Le Guin?*

There was once an old lady who was said to be a fairy, and was thus much in demand as a godmother. She had so many god-daughters that she lost count of them; but she was good-natured and conscious of her duty, and when they came, every one of them in due course, to ask for a ball-dress, or three wishes, or an introduction to an unmarried prince, she did her best for them.

She disliked being known as a fairy, for she was really a mistress of illusion. Having been disappointed in love when she was a girl, she had developed her natural talent in this line, and had been able to help a good many god-daughters in this simple way. She could easily make a plain cotton dress look like the most sumptuous of ball-gowns, a few rain-drops look like diamonds, and even half-a-dozen mice look like ponies if necessary. This was all very well for a short time, and ball-gowns are put away next morning; but if a god-daughter tried to take sensible thought for her future by selling the diamonds, they were simply rain-drops. As for the mice, they of course were under no illusion and, as well as tired to death by pulling even a small carriage, they were apt to get resentful at being kept in harness until midnight; and the old lady (whose name was Plaisance) saw no reason to indulge god-daughters at the expense of mice. What was more to the point was that she was very rich. Unless time was short, it was easier to buy a ball-gown than create the illusion of one, the more so that, not being herself a great lover of balls, she was not always abreast of fashion; she had known a god-daughter burst into tears to find herself suddenly enclosed in boned white satin with slashed sleeves and a farthingale, when no one that year would be seen in anything but the loosest of silk muslin with *coquelicot* ribbons. And, though she liked to be sure that she could work with anything she had to hand, she soon found that it created fewer problems to do things in the normal way. She *could* make a carriage out of a pumpkin; but it caused a terrible flurry in the kitchen if she called for a pumpkin when the chef knew that she did not like pumpkin pie, and it was much simpler to order her own carriage to be made ready.

She was saddened, as the years went by, because the god-daughters, nice girls though they were, once they had had their three wishes went away, generally only reappearing married to their princes and asking her to be godmother to their daughters. It would have been nicer, she sometimes thought, if they visited her more often but with less reason, but after her disappointment in love she had withdrawn to her castle, and was probably too dull for young people. So she kept herself busy looking after her estates and her people, and when she had time to spare kept her illusions in trim. There is no harm in making a mouse look like a pony so long as you do not ask it to do a pony's work, and she enjoyed having them running round her gardens. It looked, in any case, as if she would not have much else to do until the next generation of god-children grew up, for all the available princes were now married, most of them to her god-daughters.

One summer's day, however, there appeared at her door a girl with worn shoes and a bundle in her hand, who dropped a curtsey and said in a shy voice that her step-mother was cruel to her and she had come to ask shelter of her godmother.

"I am ashamed to say," said Plaisance, "that I have no recollection of you at all. What is your name, my dear?"

"I am Fennena of Doucecoeur, my lady," said the girl, and dropped another curtsey. Her manners were charming, and so was she, with a great flaxen plait over one shoulder; but somehow Plaisance could not remember that name.

"Doucecoeur?" she said. "Now I know the family, but surely the daughters were much younger than me?"

"Oh yes," said Fennena, looking earnestly up at her. "My mother was the eldest. She was the youngest girl in your finishing-school when you were the oldest. She often told me how she used to brush your hair for you."

Although she was a little wisp of a thing with round pink cheeks, Fennena's eyes were greenish-grey and narrow and very direct. As they gazed at her, Plaisance began to have a faint memory of another little wisp of a thing who had brushed her hair for her at school. Nevertheless, she had been sure that there were no god-daughters unaccounted for. "Tell me," she said, "about your christening."

Fennena dropped her gaze and said, "You weren't there, my lady. My mother died the week after I was born, and it was a very quiet christening, and you asked my father to stand in for you. Now he has married again, and has two daughters he loves more than me."

"Then that accounts for it," said Plaisance kindly, and rang for her maid. "Edith, this is my god-daughter Fennena of Doucecoeur. Will you look after her? A bath and fresh clothes and lunch in her room; we can talk when she is rested."

Edith came back presently and said in her scolding voice, "That girl is no more a god-daughter than I am."

Plaisance was sitting at the side of her pool, throwing bread to the swans. She was amusing herself by turning them into miniature galleons. It was a pretty illusion at a distance, but when they came up for bread you could see that her knowledge of the rigging was vague; they did not revert to being swans, but now and then they degenerated into junks. "That is an ill-timed remark," she said. "I am quite as fond of you, Edith, as of any god-daughter."

"And have been quite as good to me as to any god-daughter," said Edith; "but that's neither here nor there. What I'm telling you is that that girl is a brazen hussy who's out to make what she can from you. Don't say I didn't warn you."

It was true that, now Fennena's narrow greenish-grey eyes were not on her, Plaisance's memory of a little girl brushing her hair was fading rapidly; but she was not a mistress of illusion for nothing. After lunch she went to the room they had given Fennena. They had given her a new dress too, and she was looking at herself in the mirror, and she did not look quite as shy as at first. Plaisance stood at the door, and she put two of her ten finger-tips together in a certain way and spoke words of disspelling. She saw that the flaxen plait was dyed and the pink cheeks rouged, and the pretty mouth firm and hard. And, because she was in front of the mirror, Fennena saw it too.

She stared at herself for a time, and then she laughed. "Well, I knew what I looked like," she said, "and that's more than you can say of most. Did you never disspell any of your god-daughters?"

Plaisance had not; but it came into her mind that one or two of them had certainly used make-up and that all of them had been on their best behaviour to her. She said mildly, "But you are not a god-daughter and I never knew your mother."

"And why should I suffer for it?" said Fennena. "Their mothers got your help for them because they were greedy. Why shouldn't I do my own asking?"

"And show your own greed?" said Plaisance.

"Didn't I say I knew what I looked like?" said Fennena. And her small narrow-eyed face in the mirror was greedy enough. But Plaisance saw that it was not silly; and some of the god-daughters, standing there waiting for their three wishes, had really looked very silly.

"Come and walk with me in the garden," she said.

They walked through the lime avenue to the pool. Plaisance had forgotten to turn the galleons back into swans, and they looked very odd, paddling in their stately fashion one way while their sails blew out the other way. Fennena said scornfully, "I couldn't do that illusion, but I would have thought of the wind."

"Yes," said Plaisance nodding, "I thought you had talents of illusion. You very nearly spelled me into believing in your mother. Do you want to learn illusions?"

"No," said Fennena. She added grudgingly, "Well, I wouldn't mind learning one or two. But what I want is to marry the King."

Plaisance was shocked. "The King is too old for you. He is a grandfather."

"He's a widower," said Fennena, "and there's no reason why he shouldn't marry again. And I want him to marry me."

"It would be quite improper," said Plaisance. "I see the force of your argument about my god-daughters, and since you were enterprising enough to come and ask I agree that there is no good reason why I shouldn't help you. But not to marry the King. If it had been a prince now – but all the princes are married."

"If it had been a prince I'd have managed for myself," said Fennena. "If I can almost spell you into believing you knew my mother, then I can spell any prince into thinking me as beautiful as the next girl. But there are plenty of princesses, and I want to be Queen. And girls like me never meet kings."

"I used to know the King well," said Plaisance, "though it is – I forget how many years it is since we met. I assure you that you would have no chance at all of marrying him even with the help of every illusion I am mistress of. You can do a little in the illusion line yourself. You know how useless illusions are in the long run."

"Rain-drops that are diamonds for a night," Fennena said crisply, "are of little use to a lady who has plenty of diamonds by day. And if you are so sure the King won't marry me, where's the harm in letting me try? Look," she added impatiently, "do think of something more sensible for that poor bird." And she turned the galleon into a gondola.

She could hold the illusion firm for only a minute, but it certainly looked more sensible, drifting on the still water, than the galleon with its sails blowing the wrong way.

"You have talent," Plaisance admitted. "But you can't see the King in the summer. He goes to his castle in the south, and I don't visit him there nowadays. You'll have to wait until the Court comes back in the autumn. Suppose I take that time to teach you a little more about spelling?" For she thought that with time, and perhaps some easy living and a small present at the end, Fennena would forget the foolish idea of being Queen. But also, having a respect for her own art of illusion, she did not like to see so promising a newcomer lost for the want of a teacher.

"I don't mind," said Fennena. "And I might make myself useful about the place."

For it must be admitted that since the marriage of the last

god-daughter, with no more need for balls and visits to Court, Plaisance and her people had perhaps let their way of life become too easy. Edith had given up making sure that her mistress had fashionable clothes, for if a neighbouring duchess did drop in unexpectedly it needed only a spell to make a gardening dress into a silk gown. Bertrand the steward and Jacob the head gardener spent a great deal of their time playing chess. What did it matter if the grand salon had not been spring-cleaned for three years, when it was never used, or if the fountains in the terraced garden did not work?

"It matters that half the girls in the village are out of work," snapped Fennena, and needed no illusions to send Bertrand running to engage them for spring-cleaning at three silver pennies a week. He thought the going rate was two silver pennies a week, but Fennena soon put him right about that. To Jacob she said, "Old Ben's second son in the village will know how to mend fountains," and to Edith, "There isn't a piece of lace in this chest that isn't torn – send for Betty's daughters from the village to mend it."

"I would much rather that you didn't upset Edith," said Plaisance when they met at dinner in the evening.

"Edith can afford to be upset," said Fennena. "She has a good job, assured for life. Betty's third daughter can't afford to marry Old Ben's second son unless you give them work."

Plaisance opened her eyes in surprise. "But if they had told me I would have given them what they need."

"They'd rather have the work," said Fennena shortly; "and old gardens and good lace don't deserve neglect. That pudding in front of you is apples from your orchard baked in honey from your hives. Why do you have to make it look like crystallised fruits from Arabia? You know it will still taste like apples."

"A silly habit," said Plaisance, and hastily put two finger-tips together and restored the pudding to its rightful appearance. She was becoming a little intimidated by Fennena, for she added apologetically, "I don't at all like crystallised fruits from Arabia."

"Don't you?" said Fennena. "I've never tasted them. I suppose in Arabia they make their crystallised fruits look like honey-baked apples. And another thing. If I'm to tidy up this castle you've got to get rid of all these illusions you keep leaving around."

"Fennena," said Plaisance bravely, "you are going too far. I can have illusions in my own castle if I like them."

"But do you like them?" said Fennena. "That one over there, for example;" and she pointed to the end wall of the middle-sized dining-hall in which they were having dinner. With two of them, they did not use the small dining-hall, which was only forty feet long, but the middle-sized one, which left such a length of table between them that they had to speak distinctly. But these days Fennena's voice was much more distinct than Plaisance's, not at all the voice of the shy girl in the worn shoes who had come to the castle at the beginning of summer.

"There is nothing wrong with that illusion," said Plaisance defensively. She had called it into existence one evening when a countess had stayed to dinner and it had occurred to her that the middle-sized dining-hall, which she had not seen for some months, was very dark at one end.

"Nothing *wrong*!" said Fennena. "A view of a beech-wood in autumn is a nice idea, but why did you put children picking primroses into it? And that child on the left repeats himself every three minutes and the clouds don't move at all."

"I think it very pretty," said Plaisance, and left her honey-baked apples half-eaten and went up to her room. Edith came to help her undress, and said jealously, "It's that girl has made your cry, my lady. Send her away."

Plaisance would very much have liked to send Fennena away, except that she was proving such a good maid of illusions. And it came into her mind that, after all, Edith had indeed a good job assured for life, and that the illusion in the middle-sized dining-hall had been conjured up too quickly. She had meant, once the countess had gone, to do the job properly, but somehow it had never seemed worth while. She said, "Miss Fennena is only doing as I asked her, Edith, and don't you think this night-dress needs mending around the cuffs?" And she made up her mind that next morning she would go to the middle-sized dining-hall and make a proper illusion at the dark end.

Next morning Edith brought in her breakfast with pinched lips, and took away a pile of mending with a very martyred air. Plaisance went towards the middle-sized dining-hall, but on the way noticed that she had left an illusion about on one of the landings. She had been reading a book about Greek statues at the time, and had thought it would be nice to have one in the castle, but her recollection of the illustrations had been a little mixed; she had left it there because she knew what she meant if no one else did. She wiped it out as she passed, and thought of wiping out also the illusion of a Gobelin tapestry in the fourth vestibule; but it seemed to her that that illusion, though perhaps not Gobelin, was quite pretty. Or would have been pretty if time had not leaked into it, letting the wall of the fourth vestibule show through at several points. She put two finger-tips together and restored the fading parts, and then saw a place in the upper right-hand corner where she had forgotten to put any pattern at all. She put two more finger-tips together to sketch in some ideas. Interlacing trees with deer disappearing into them? No, there were deer in the foreground. Rabbits, then? The rabbits were not quite tall enough for her space, so she added some greenery, and then discovered that she had not a clear idea of the kind of greenery that rabbits lived in. Forgetting about the middle-sized dining-hall, she took a sketch-book and pencil into the garden and spent such a time drawing greenery of different kinds that it was lunch-time before she knew it. Fennena, who had taken command in the most unlikely places, had had a picnic set at the edge of the gardens, where they could look out over the estate, and half-way through the chicken sandwiches Plaisance said, "Of course! A stream-bank with sally willows along it!" and put down her sandwich and began to draw it.

"I told them to mend those fences down there," said Fennena, and looking over her shoulder added, "That tatty thing in the fourth vestibule – yes, that might do. Gillian in the village can weave it."

"I was designing an illusion," Plaisance said, "not a tapestry."

"It'll be better as a tapestry. You draw it out properly, and I'll get Gillian to come up and see you about it."

Next morning Gillian was setting up her loom, and trying to persuade Plaisance that her daughters, too, could weave well. Plaisance would have believed her, but Fennena said, "Your daughters couldn't touch fine details like this. You get Old Joan to help you."

And, quite bewildered by all this, Plaisance at last found time to go to the middle-sized dining-hall. She looked at the illusion there and had to agree that it was terrible. Then she remembered that Old Ben's eldest son was said to work in stained glass, and what could be better in a dark wall than a stained-glass window?

She was so pleased with the idea that she sent for Fennena and told her about it.

"Well, go on," said Fennena, "let's see what it would look like."

"You do it," said Plaisance generously, and taught her how to make the spell.

Fennena put her fingers as she was told, and there appeared in the wall a coloured window. It was a good solid window with a firm frame and shapes of good colour between black leadings, but what it was meant to be, no one could have said. Fennena tightened her fingers, and the leadings snapped like elastic into different places and the colours flicked from one space to another; but it still did not look like anything in particular.

"Now keep your mind on it," said Plaisance anxiously.

"It's no use," said Fennena. "I can do the illusion, but I can't make it look beautiful. If it's to be done, you'll have to do it."

And she and Plaisance exchanged looks.

As they did this, they both altered a little. Plaisance lost her anxious air, but Fennena's sharp frown grew less. "Yes," said Plaisance after a time, "I'll have to do it, but the design will take thought."

"I'll see when Old Ben's eldest son can do the work," said Fennena. "And don't you think Old Ben himself might start on the kitchens? They are three flights from the dining-rooms, so that Matty's cooking always gets to us cold, and that illusion of fifteen footmen to run up with the dishes is no use at all."

"I have always had fifteen footmen," said Plaisance, bewildered.

"Dear Lady Plaisance," said Fennena, "when they grew too old to run, you kindly replaced them by illusions. But illusions can only carry illusory dishes, and to carry the real dishes there is only the scullery-maid now."

Matty sometimes sent up soufflés which were cold and sunken in the middle, but out of the kindness of her heart

Plaisance spelled them to look round and perfect. The spelling made no difference to the taste, which was horrible, and it occurred to her now that the winding stair of three flights would accommodate a lift.

"Hmm. That's an idea new to the village," said Fennena. "But Barty the carpenter will try anything once."

So what it came to, during that summer, was that the castle began to hum with all kinds of work, and that Plaisance was too busy to listen to Edith's complaints, and that, while everyone agreed that the mistress was even kinder than usual, they also agreed that that girl Fennena was an overbearing nuisance.

One day at the end of August, between comparing dyes for tapestry wools and listening to Barty's new inspiration about incorporating a brass pan of charcoal in the dining-hall lift to keep the dishes hot, Plaisance recalled that it was nearly time for the Court to come back, and that she had, almost, promised that then she would let Fennena meet the King. Being a lady of her word, she called Fennena to her room to speak to her about it. But first she could not resist showing her the completed cartoon for the tapestry.

"Not bad," said Fennena grudgingly. "Though you know I've no judgement in these things. We've had an inquiry from a Baron's lady who wants to know if Gillian's girls could weave her a hunting scene, and she's offering good money."

"*Money?*" said Plaisance.

"Gillian's girls need it," Fennena said. "They need you, too, to design the tapestry, but you can't deprive them of what they could earn. And wouldn't you like to design a hunting scene?"

Plaisance in fact had some ideas about a hunting scene, and she felt warmly towards Gillian's girls, who had come on wonderfully well; but she said, "That's not what I want to talk about."

"All right," said Fennena; "but while I remember, Old Ben's eldest son is getting enquiries about more windows. I'm not too pleased with the fountain-work, but given time that will come into fashion too."

"Then perhaps you will be too busy to go to Court and see if you can make the King marry you?" said Plaisance.

Fennena looked taken aback; but said after a pause, "That's what I came here for."

"And do you think you can do it?"

Fennena turned to look at herself in the mirror. She had not worried much, lately, about keeping up her own illusions; she was an insignificant little thing but for the directness of her eyes, and that directness was not altogether pleasant. She put four finger-tips together and spoke a spell, and at once she was charming, with big shy eyes and the great flaxen plait over one shoulder. "I can try," she said. "I've learnt a great deal about illusion this summer."

"And who was your teacher?" said Plaisance, and countered the spell with only two finger-tips, and there was a very plain girl indeed in the mirror. Fennena looked at it undisturbed, and said, "You only used two finger-tips too. Well, I only used four. We'll see."

When she was at the door, Plaisance called her back, in a voice that shook a very little.

"Fennena dear, I – I did a little more than counter your spell. You are not quite as plain as I made you look."

"I know," said Fennena. "Illusions are no good against the truth, my lady."

The following week they went to Court. Once it was seen that Plaisance's town house was open, invitations began to arrive, dressmakers thronged to beg for orders, and soon the King's messengers arrived commanding her presence at his reception that evening.

"I am most happy to accept," she said to the messengers, "and beg His Majesty's permission to present to him my youngest god-daughter;" and to the dressmakers she said, "No, we don't need you. For what do two illusionists," she added to Fennena, "want with dressmakers?"

"Yes, we'll spell our dresses," said Fennena; "and you can see that *they* aren't in need of work."

So that evening they both put on comfortable old dresses and stood in front of the mirror, and Fennena said, "Do show me what you are going to wear."

"Certainly," said Plaisance, and spelled her old dress into deep rose watered silk, adding rubies to go with it.

"Very becoming," said Fennena, watching narrowly. "But why waste illusion on rubies when you have yours in the coffer over there?"

"Good gracious," said Plaisance, "it's no effort to me, and I have illusion to spare."

"Maybe," said Fennena; "but you have never designed jewellery, so you have missed the finer points of the setting."

And she spelled the rubies so that their setting – which in Plaisance's easy-going way had certainly looked a little vague – grew clear and exact.

"You are perfectly right," said Plaisance, "and since you are going to need all your powers of illusion I will have to wear my real rubies. Do them up behind, will you? And now show me what you are going to wear."

"What do you think of this?" said Fennena, and stroke by clear stroke she made herself a dazzlingly fair young girl, with great blue eyes and a gown of sky-blue flounces.

"*Far* too fussy, my dear," said Plaisance, and removed half the flounces, deepened the colour a shade, and spelled a simple string of pearls; and to show that it was no effort added just a tinge of violet to her own deep rose.

"Your taste was always better than mine," said Fennena, and without effort took over the illusion and made the pearls a better-matched string. "Shall we go?"

"Certainly," said Plaisance, and let herself be helped into her cloak with a relieved heart. For she had once known the King very well, and was quite sure that he did not care for dazzling blondes in conspicuous dresses. His Queen had been a shy dark-eyed lady who dressed quietly. Plaisance took a last look at herself in the mirror, and as an afterthought faded the colour of her gown a little more. She was proud to see that she did not have to use illusion to make her eyes as clear and dark and sparkling as they had been thirty years ago, when she had known the King so very well.

When they reached the Palace, in a long line of coaches

making for the King's reception, they went first into the cloakroom, and Fennena helped Plaisance off with her cloak, but kept her own closely drawn, with the hood over her head. All around them were ladies smoothing their skirts and plumping up their hair and talking hard.

"The King looks well," said one.

"But tired and lonely," said another. "He should marry again."

"Oh he should," agreed a third. "He deserves a good wife for his last years. Not a young girl, of course, with his three sons married, and all their wives so gay and pretty. Someone quiet and kind to make him happy."

Fennena in her cloak and hood stood still in front of the mirror, and all that could be seen of her was her two hands with four finger-tips pressed together, and Plaisance whirled on her in fear and fury.

"Stay as you are!" she whispered. "Or I will strip all illusion from you in front of the Court."

Fennena did nothing but press six finger-tips together; and in the mirror Plaisance saw, wavering into being in the shelter of the cloak and hood, a slender lady of perhaps thirty with quiet dark eyes.

"Take off that illusion!" she hissed.

"Please don't interrupt me," said Fennena, and spelled her dress to dark blue and her flaxen curls to a smooth brown knot.

Plaisance put all ten finger-tips together and spoke a word of power. For a moment all of Fennena became distorted, as though she would have wavered and drifted away; and then two more of her finger-tips came together, and at once she was clear and precise and calm. "I think dark eyes wear better, don't you?" she said.

"The Lady Plaisance and god-daughter!" announced the major-domo, and Plaisance turned on her heel and joined the line of ladies that moved slowly up towards the King. The princes, who were all married to her god-daughters, came to greet her and give her news of their children, and she saw that each of them as they talked looked with curiosity over her shoulder, to where she knew that Fennena must be standing; but she neither offered to introduce her nor looked round at her. Instead she moved steadily towards the King, whom she had once known so well, knowing that she must present to him the illusion of exactly the woman he wanted for his wife, and that Fennena's powers of spelling were now stronger than her own powers of disspelling. And she thought, too, that although her own eyes were still as clear and dark as they had been thirty years ago, her face was wrinkled and her hair grown grey.

Then it was her turn to curtsey to the King, and without looking up she said, "Sir, may I present the latest of my god-daughters, Fennena of Doucecoeur." Beneath her lowered eyelids she saw a dark blue skirt billow and slide as Fennena sank in her curtsey, and saw her two hands come out with all ten finger-tips together, and felt the shiver that comes over the world of the mistress of illusions when one of the words of power is spoken; and then there was an odd silence.

When at last Plaisance looked up, there was the Court watching enthralled, while the King held out his hands to her, and his expression was exactly as it had been the first time they had met, thirty years ago, the day before it was decided that for reasons of state he must marry the shy dark-eyed lady who became Queen; and he was taking no notice at all of the insignificant little thing at her side, in a dark-blue dress that did not suit her.

So Plaisance and the King were married, and for a wedding present Fennena gave them a complete set of faked Gobelin tapestries. They had to be faked because she could not design tapestries herself, so she studied them in illustrated books and made illusions of them for Gillian and her girls to weave. The complete set of fountains which Plaisance's people at the castle gave them was a fair half Fennena's present too; they would never have got them right if it had not been for her overbearing ways.

"But I *saw* you making an illusion at the moment we met the King," Plaisance said to her when they could be alone. "It was a most powerful spell too; I've never see you use ten fingers before. What was it?"

"That wasn't a spell," said Fennena, "it was a counter-spell. I took off all illusions, so that the King saw us exactly as we were. It was a very powerful spell indeed," she added reflectively. "I don't suppose you noticed any of the Court ladies just then, but nearly all of them lost something of their looks."

"But to disspell everything!" said Plaisance, professionally distressed. "And Fennena, I have never known a more powerful mistress of illusion than you. To waste all your talent!"

"I can do illusions pretty well," said Fennena, "but somehow I like disillusions better now. I seem to get more satisfaction out of them. And though it's very kind of you and the King to ask me, I don't think I'll stay at Court after the wedding. There's such a lot to be done at the castle with all these orders coming in, and I do hope you'll find time soon to design us some more windows. Old Ben's eldest son is developing some beautiful new colours for his glass."

Plaisance was so happy married to the King that she designed them both windows and tapestries. The Castle Crafts became famous and no one was ever out of work in the village. She was so happy that it never occurred to her to wonder why, when Fennena made her great disspelling, she had found it necessary to use a word of power as well as all ten finger-tips. Fennena never told her that that had been to hold one illusion steady in the midst of all the disillusion; she had made Plaisance look thirty instead of fifty. She had been prepared to defend this to the King, but as he never seemed to notice any discrepancy afterwards, she kept quiet about it. The only person who ever heard the story was Old Ben's eldest son, to whom, after refusing several offers from ambitious courtiers, she was married three or four years later. Young Ben said, "I shouldn't worry about him; you can see he's all right. What I'd like to know is something much more a puzzle than that."

"I suppose you've got to," said Fennena.

"The way you tell it, you were set on being Queen until the very last moment. What changed your mind? Now don't tell me it was your sweet nature, because I know you too well."

"Would I be such a fool?" said Fennena. "The truth was that they'd told me what kind of a wife the King wanted, and I was spelling myself into just that. And the nearer I got to it the more I looked like Plaisance."

THE ANKLET

from

THE ARABIAN NIGHTS

retold by

NAOMI LEWIS

"Cinderella", in its familiar form, comes to us by way of courtly Perrault (for more of him, see the Introduction). Sadly, it has been coarsened somewhat over the centuries. In Perrault, the older sisters were vain and haughty: they were not vulgar and stupid pantomime harridans. Nor did they chop lumps off their feet in hope of fitting the shoe. But, did you know that, over the world, there are hundreds of different versions of this story? "The Anklet" here is an Eastern variant. What are the differences? For a start, the three sisters are all working girls, an oddly modern touch. They earn their living by spinning. There is no pumpkin carriage – indeed, there's no fairy godmother. An

*alabaster pot supplies the needed magic. The quaintest difference con-
cerns the royal ball. Only men are present; the women have their party
in the harem. So the prince never even sees our heroine, the "dazzling
stranger" in her finery. But he does find the tiny diamond anklet that
the girl loses in her haste to reach home before her sisters; and this
prompts the royal search. The horses, at least, know that magic is
involved. They snort with fear when they see the anklet lying in their
water trough – a curiously effective detail.*

L egends tell that long ago, in a certain city, there
were three sisters, who lived by spinning flax. All
had the same father, but the youngest was the child
of a second wife. And though all three were like the moon
in beauty, the youngest had the fairest face and a charm of
manner that both the others lacked. What's more, she was
a faster and finer spinner than either; not a single fault
could be found in the thread that left her hand. As you may
imagine, the sisters did not love this favoured girl, no,
indeed they did not, and they suffered much from jealousy.

One day the youngest one was in the market, buying the
day's supplies, when her eye was caught by a little alabaster
pot, and she bought it from her spinning money. With a few
flowers inside, she thought, it would give her pleasure to glance
at while she worked. But her sisters looked at it scornfully.

"What extravagance!" said one.

"What a silly waste of money!" said the other. The girl felt
sad, and was silent. She put a rose in the pot, set it in front of
her, and went back to her spinning.

Now this was no ordinary pot; it had magic powers, as the young girl soon discovered. When she wished to eat, it brought her delicious food; when she longed for lovely clothes, it laid before her shimmering silken robes that any princess might envy. Still, she had the sense not to reveal this secret to her sisters, and she passed the days as before, saying little, spinning much, and always dressing soberly. But whenever the two went out to enjoy themselves, she shut herself in her own little room and tenderly clasped the treasure.

"Little pot, dear little pot," she would say, "I beg you to bring me—" and then she would add whatever her fancy lit on at the moment. And at once she would find before her dazzling jewels, lustrous fabrics, delicious cakes and fruits, sweets of fine-spun sugar, as ravishing to look upon as to taste. But as soon as it heard the sound of the sisters' feet, the good little pot would make all traces vanish; there was the girl, spinning away, and there before her was the pot, holding a single rose. In this way many weeks passed. When other people were present, the youngest appeared to be just a poor working girl. But when she was alone, she was a princess, lacking for nothing.

One day the king announced that he was giving a great feast, and inviting all the householders of the city. Among these were the three sisters. But the two older girls had their own views on that. They told the youngest to stay at home to mind the house; then they dressed as well as they could from a spinner's wage, and set off for the palace. As soon as they were out of sight, the young girl spoke sweetly to the pot, then asked to be given clothes so beautiful that she would outshine all at the feast.

"And I beg you too, little pot," she added, "for turquoise bracelets for my arms, sapphire and amethyst rings for my fingers, and little diamond anklets for my feet." At once these things were before her. Hastily she dressed herself and made her way to the harem part of the palace, where the women were allowed their own entertainment.

All the assembled guests, her sisters among them, marvelled at the beauty of this dazzling stranger – surely a high princess. But the girl thought it best to leave before the end; and while the women gathered to listen to an entertainment of singers, she slipped away leaping over the sunken water trough where the royal horses came to drink, and swiftly glided home. There she was, quietly waiting in her mended clothes when the older pair returned. She did not know that in her haste she had dropped a diamond anklet in the trough.

Next morning when the palace horses were taken to drink, they backed away in terror, snorting and trembling, stamping with their hooves. The grooms looked down and saw a shining thing in the water, a ring of stars, it seemed; it was the diamond anklet.

The king's son, who had been watching the strange behaviour of his horses, looked at it curiously, then cried out, "Only the rarest of damsels could wear a thing so small, so exquisite. She is the one I shall marry and none other!" He went to his royal father and told him of his decision.

"As you will, my son," replied he monarch. "But really, I know very little about these things. Your mother is the one to go to; she'll help you to find the girl." So the prince went to his mother and showed her the anklet.

"I am determined to marry the girl with the incredible ankle," he said, "and I put the matter in your hands, for my father says that you understand these things."

"I hear and obey," said the queen, and at once she called her women together to plan the search for the damsel. Harem after harem they visited, up and down the city, but nowhere could they find a girl whose ankle matched the jewel. One week passed, then another. They were just about to admit defeat when they came upon the modest home of the spinning sisters. The first two proffered their feet, but with no success at all. Then the youngest asked to try, and the anklet at once slipped on as if it were part of her.

"Well now, our quest is at an end, and I am glad of that," said the queen, who was quite exhausted. "She seems a charming girl as well, and the prettiest we've seen, I do believe." She embraced the happy damsel, and the wedding date was announced; there were feastings and celebrations for forty days and nights.

And where were the older sisters all this time? They too were in the palace, for the goodhearted bride had invited them to share in all the merrymaking. Happiness made her careless, though, and on the fortieth day she revealed to them the secret of the pot, which had even helped with her wedding clothes. The women whispered together, then offered to arrange her hair. They combed the long tresses, coiled them round and held them in place with seven diamond pins. But these were enchanted pins, which they had obtained from the alabaster pot; their power was to turn a human maiden into a dove. And when the last pin was inserted, no girl was there, only a white bird, which flew in fright through the window. The prince came to find his bride – but where was she? Not a trace of her could be seen.

"She told us that she was off for a stroll in the garden," said the sisters, putting on anxious looks and glancing hither and thither. Search parties were sent through the grounds then through the city, then throughout the kingdom. The king sent ships to the farthest shores of his domain, seeking for news of his son's vanished bride. But the lost girl was not found, and the prince began to waste away; in his anguish and bitterness he refused to leave his room. So sunk in grief was he that at first he took no notice of a little dove that came to his window every morning and evening. Then he began to take comfort in the bird, and to watch for its coming. One day he put out his hand and the bird alighted on his palm. He began to stroke her softly, but his hand met several hard little objects, like the heads of pins. And pins they were. One by one he pulled them forth, and when the last was drawn, a mist obscured the dove for a moment; it seemed to vanish – and then before him was a lovely girl, his lost bride found, none other.

No more misfortunes crossed the path of the prince and the princess. They lived in happiness ever after, and their children were many and beautiful. But when the sisters saw that their plot had failed, their rage rushed into their hearts, and so they died.

THE TULIP BED

by

WILLIAM MAYNE

William Mayne's achievement here – or one of them – is to write about fairy people of the old traditional kind, yet to place them in a fresh new story; quite unlike any other. Well, no one can match this outstanding writer for plots. How does his work have such an air of entire conviction? You don't question its happenings. Partly this comes from his exact attention to facts, something needed as much in fantasy as in other matters. Maybe more. We know why the good Dutchman has come to England; we know what is planted in the garden; and that the little door – a master touch – will also have its keys. So when Mayne tells us that these pixies in Blackheath were the last ever seen in London (as so often, they were driven out by the Church) we know that this is so. A perfect story; a perfect piece of storytelling.

A Dutchman called Deventer, and his family came to live at the edge of Blackheath. The Mynheer was serving the King here on some business with ships and from there he could get down to the river.

He had a house belonging to the King, but it wanted more garden, which Dutchmen like, so he took in a square of heath, which the King granted him. It was meant to be for his lifetime only, because the commoners of the heath had a right to it.

He had a high brick wall built round it, because Dutch gardens are very private and folk looking in over fences spoil it for them. He had a door through on to Blackheath, if he wanted to walk there.

Then he dug the plot over with his own spade. He said there were no gardeners skilled enough in London. He laid it out in squares and rounds and put in his plants, and the folk near by knew he was growing onions in some fancy way not in neat rows. But that's the way with foreign gentlemen.

Then he was complaining to the King about his neighbours banging at his garden gate day and night, and when he got to it no one was there. The King said he must catch them at it. But the Dutchman never saw any person.

But the parson there knew who was at the door, even if knowing it wasn't church law. He said it was the pixies and that Mynheer Deventer had enclosed one of their grounds and kept them out of it. He collected old tales, he said.

Mynheer Deventer said *Yah* very many times, because he was in a foreign country and things were different. He called the bricklayers back, and a carpenter, and they built a very little door beside his own Dutchman-sized one, and he locked it and hung the keys beside it, thinking the pixies would understand.

They did, and next morning the keys had gone. But the banging stopped, and the garden was peaceful.

His garden grew. How high a wall doesn't matter, because folk will stand on each other's shoulders to spy over the top. So it was known how the garden grew very pretty in a year or two with the new flower called Turkshead, or tulip, very fresh to the country that year. The garden was full of them, yellow and red and brown, filling all the squares and rounds and garden-bed shapes, among the little bushes of box and other sweet shrubs.

This is what Mynheer Deventer told the King. By the little door there was a gate-keeper pixy, which no man could see, but it kept away cats and dogs and weasels and stoats and any harmful thing, only letting in and out the young pixy mothers with their babes.

Also, the Mynheer said, these were the only tulips in the world to have a sweet scent all night long.

It is not known what the King thought.

The parson, and one or two local gentlemen, and their ladies were let into the house to see the garden closer. They smelled the flowers, and late in the evening they also heard some sort of sound.

The King's master of song came, and heard music. He wrote down a few lines of tune, and they could be heard whistled in the city for a year or two.

He would have written some of it for church, but the, bishops would not let him use pixy melody.

These grand people heard a little and smelled somewhat, but only the Mynheer's children saw what else there was.

They wrote it down later, but the parson said they had made it up from what he had said about old tales. But the children said that the old tales were proved.

The garden was a nursery, they said, and the flowers made music to rest the babes while the mothers slept and rested, combed their hair, and mended their wings. Then they kissed their babies, and in the morning early they would troop out of the garden back to their homes hidden on the heath.

Mynheer and Mynfrow believed them, but the parson wrote to the King that these people were not acting like Christians. The King remembered what he had been told by the Mynheer about the gate-keeper pixy, and said the Mynheer and his family must go, and back to Holland they went. That was before that war, but did not cause it.

Then, instead of taking the wall down and giving back that enclosed piece of Blackheath, which he had promised the commoners he would do, the King let a park-keeper live in the house and grow herbs for the King's table. So the tulips went, and there was parsley instead, and onions, as was first supposed, in long rows.

And he broke down the little door so that his dogs could

come in and out. All these things made the garden no longer a nursery, and perhaps a pixy had been hurt or a baby killed in the new work, or the ground was now dangerous. But from that time on the parsley drooped and withered, the onions rotted as they grew, and at last there was only the black soil and no living thing.

In time the pixies left the whole of the heath, and they were the last pixies in the whole of London. This was a few hundred years ago.

It is said that the graves of a certain family in Holland are tended by unseen hands, and that on them grow small tulips, of an old kind that have a scent. No other tulips have that. But if they are picked the scent goes at once. Perhaps that is where the pixies went, and the graves are those of Mynheer Deventer and his family who had been kind to them.

As for the garden at Blackheath, the house has long gone, and the brick wall is a shadow on the turf, and inside no strange flowers grow. Only now and then on a dewy morning the pattern of the old garden shows on the ground until the sun dries it away.

THE KING
O' THE CATS

by
JOSEPH JACOBS

*With its mounting tension and crack of its eerie climax, this little rustic
teaser should be told, ideally, by winter evening firelight, to properly
attentive listeners. It comes from Joseph Jacobs's* More English Fairy
Tales *(1894), the successor to his* English Fairy Tales *of 1889, and in his
own opinion "surpassing the former in interest and vivacity". Maybe it
does have more "discoveries". Our story here has a curious back-
ground. "Five versions of this quaint legend," notes the genial Jacobs,
"have been collected in England." (He gives the references.) The familiar version here is his assembling from these five – so don't attempt to
place it locally. In further comment, Jacobs calls it "an interesting*

example of the speed and development of a simple anecdote throughout England . . . [For] we can scarcely imagine more than a single origin to the tale, which in its way" (he adds) "is as weird and fantastic as Edgar Allan Poe."

It is best not to read or tell this tale in the presence of a cat.

O ne winter's evening the sexton's wife was sitting by the fireside with her big black cat, Old Tom, on the other side, both half asleep and waiting for the master to come home. They waited and they waited, but still he didn't come, till at last he came rushing in, calling out, "Who's Tommy Tildrum?" in such a wild way that both his wife and his cat stared at him to know what was the matter.

"Why, what's the matter?" said his wife. "And why do you want to know who Tommy Tildrum is?"

"Oh, I've had such an adventure. I was digging away at old Mr Fordyce's grave when I suppose I must have dropped asleep, and only woke up by hearing a cat's *Miaou.*"

"*Miaou!*" said Old Tom in answer.

"Yes, just like that! So I looked over the edge of the grave, and what do you think I saw?"

"Now, how can I tell?" said the sexton's wife.

"Why, nine black cats all like our friend Tom here, all with a white spot on their chestesses. And what do you think they were carrying? Why, a small coffin covered with a black velvet pall, and on the pall was a small coronet all of gold, and at every third step they took they cried all together, *Miaou*—"

"Miaou!" said Old Tom again.

"Yes; just like that!" said the sexton. "And as they came nearer and nearer to me I could see them more distinctly, because their eyes shone out with a sort of green light. Well, they all came towards me, eight of them carrying the coffin and the biggest cat of all walking in front for all the world like . . . But look at our Tom, how he's looking at me. You'd think he knew all I was saying."

"Go on, go on," said his wife; "never mind Old Tom."

"Well, as I was a-saying, they came towards me slowly and solemnly, and at every third step crying all together, *Miaou*—"

"Miaou!" said Old Tom again.

"Yes; just like that; till they came and stood right opposite Mr Fordyce's grave, where I was, when they all stood still and looked straight at me. I did feel queer, that I did! But look at Old Tom; he's looking at me just like they did."

"Go on, go on," said his wife; "never mind Old Tom."

"Where was I? Oh, they all stood still looking at me, when the one that wasn't carrying the coffin came forward and staring straight at me, said to me – yes, I tell 'ee, *said* to me – with a squeaky voice, 'Tell Tom Tildrum that Tim Toldrum's dead,' and that's why I asked you if you knew who Tom Tildrum was, for how can I tell Tom Tildrum Tim Toldrum's dead if I don't know who Tom Tildrum is?"

"Look at Old Tom! Look at Old Tom!" screamed his wife.

And well he might look, for Tom was swelling, and Tom was staring, and at last Tom shrieked out, "What – old Tim dead! Then I'm the King o' the Cats!" and rushed up the chimney and was never more seen.

THE FIREBIRD

by

ALEXANDER AFANASIEV

retold by

JAMES MAYHEW

If any tale needs the reminder that there is no absolute version of a traditional story, it is this. Every telling varies in its detail. In its best known form today (as here) it links two separate Russian tales from the Alexander Afanasiev collection of the 1860s, "The Firebird" and "The Death of Kastchey the Deathless". What brought these together? In brief, the Stravinsky ballet at the start of this century. Then again, Afanasiev's Firebird certainly has echoes of "The Golden Bird" in

Grimm. The basic plot of that earlier tale is much the same, but there the Emperor is a mere king, the wolf is a fox, and the "hero" a peasant boy. Would this have been so well received at the Imperial Russian Court?

But here it is, tremendous stuff – a fairy tale in the grand Russian style, and it thrives on superlatives. A princess must be of Inexhaustible Loveliness. One Emperor is not enough; there are three. Each one, possessing more than the mind can imagine, desires the unattainable. It is attained – with, of course, magic help for the sometimes bungling prince. That bringer of magic help, the Wolf, deserves a special attention – not only because, without him, there would be no story. Too long abused and ridiculed in nursery lore, here he is given what might be called the noblest role in the tale. Nor does he turn out to be just an ordinary prince in disguise – a weak negation of itself that the fox in "The Golden Bird" has to suffer. Ride with him through the landscape. "The high mountains and deep blue lakes, green forests and golden cities of old Mother Russia raced by, for the wolf all but flew. Whether or not it was a long time who knows? For a deed takes time, but a tale is quickly told."

Imagine a garden where each flower or tree was made of jewels or precious stones. The shrubs had emerald leaves. Diamonds grew there and silver roses. Their equal could not be found in any tsardom in Russia. But the rarest tree of all was just a rather small, simple apple tree, for each autumn this tree bore fruit of gold.

This was the garden of Tsar Dadon and naturally he watched over it with a keen eye. He was especially careful with the apple tree, for its fruits were dearer to him than any other jewel in his enchanted garden. That is why, one morning, he noticed that a golden apple had been stolen during the night.

Now, the tsar trusted no one except his three sons, Dmitri, Fyodor and Ivan. He called them to his throne room and told them, in a whisper, about the theft.

"Whichever one of you catches the night-time thief can have half of my tsardom," he said.

"I am the eldest, let me catch the thief," said Dmitri. He badly wanted half of his father's valuable tsardom.

All night long he sat by the tree and waited for the thief. But no one came and the glistening garden of riches was silent. Finally, Dmitri saw a glow in the sky, towards the east.

"At last! It is morning," he sighed and, believing the tree to be safe, he allowed his eyes to close for a single moment. But when he opened them again, the sky was black once more. And when he looked at the magical tree he saw that an apple had been taken.

The Tsar's second son, Fyodor, was also eager to gain half his father's tsardom. The next night he sat by the tree determined to remain awake. Just as it seemed he could no longer do so, he saw a warm glow on the eastern horizon.

"Thank goodness! It is morning," said Fyodor and he allowed his eyes to close for a half moment. But when he opened them it was dark night again and another apple had gone.

Ivan, the Tsar's youngest son, cared little for half of the tsardom but wanted to set his beloved father's mind at rest.

So the next night Ivan sat by the apple tree and fought against the sleep that pressed down on him like a heavy blanket. And so strong willed was he that he did not close his eyes once, not even when the sky grew pale in the east.

But it was not the sun that made the heavens catch fire. Across the sky, like a comet, came the Firebird. Glowing brightly, she settled on the magic tree and began to eat a golden apple.

Quickly, quietly, Ivan stole up behind the fabulous creature, stretched on his toes, and took hold of the Firebird's tail. It burned! But Ivan was brave and he held his grip.

"Please do not harm me, Tsarevich!" cried the Firebird and, as she flew upwards, a single feather fell from her tail into Ivan's scorched hand. It no longer burned but flashed and glowed all shades of gold in the first brightness of dawn.

"Take this feather in exchange for the apples," said the Firebird. "If I ever take it back, I will serve you with my life."

Then the Firebird spread her glorious burning wings and flew out of sight.

Ivan ran off at once to show the Firebird's gift to the tsar. The tsar, however, decided that the feather was not enough. "I must have this fabulous creature," he said. "She will be my prisoner, for taking the golden apples."

But the Firebird never returned to the tsar's garden. However many nights the three tsarevich-princes sat and watched, they never saw the bird again. The tsar could neither eat nor sleep. "You shall have half of my tsardom if you can find the Firebird," he said to his three sons.

Dmitri, jealous of Ivan's success, set off at once, determined to win half the tsardom. But when, after a month, he failed to return, Fyodor went in search of the magical bird, for he was as greedy as Dmitri and just as jealous of Ivan.

Another month passed, but neither brother returned. So Ivan took it upon himself to follow his brothers, despite the pleas of his father, who thought he was too young.

"Go if you must," said the tsar, "but take the Firebird's feather and place it in your cap. May it bring you good fortune."

Ivan saddled up his horse and set off. He soon reached a crossroads where a notice read: "Go back and fail, go forward and starve, go left and be eaten by wolves, go right and your horse will be eaten."

Ivan rode ahead, unafraid of hunger. But his horse was a noble animal, who turned around and galloped to the right.

No sooner had the horse done so than a large grey wolf leapt out of the forest and attacked and ate Ivan's horse.

For three days and three nights the young tsarevich wept over the bones of his trusted companion. Finally, Grey Wolf took pity on Ivan, stole up and licked his face.

"Can I not ease your sorrow, for it was I who caused it?"

"Alas, my horse is gone, and I have no way of finding the Firebird, which my father, Tsar Dadon, pines for."

"Then climb upon my back, for I know where to find the Firebird," said the wolf. "I am strong and can carry you and will be your faithful servant." Ivan did as he was told and Grey Wolf raced off at a great speed.

The high mountains and deep blue lakes, green forests and golden cities of old Mother Russia raced by, for the wolf all but flew. Whether or not it was a long time who knows? For a deed takes time but a tale is quickly told. At last they stopped in front of the great palace of Tsar Afron, which was surrounded by a high wall.

"Beyond the wall you will find the Firebird in a jewelled cage," said Grey Wolf. "Take the bird but leave the cage."

Ivan stood on the wolf's back, climbed the wall and jumped into a garden on the other side. It was full of light for at the very centre, in a magnificent cage, was the Firebird. Ivan was about to take the bird when he remembered his burnt hand and thought, "Surely if I can take the bird without being seen, I can take her cage too." So he carefully lifted the cage down from where it hung.

All at once the bells in the palace towers rang out, for the cage was tied to them by a thousand invisible threads. Guards appeared as if from nowhere and they dragged Ivan to Tsar Afron.

"You are an unlikely thief," bellowed the tsar, who could see Ivan was a nobleman. "Explain yourself!"

"Sire, I am the son of Tsar Dadon, and I took the bird, for she stole my father's golden apples," said Ivan.

"Had you come to me with your father's name to ask for the bird I should have given her to you, but to steal her and her cage is a severe crime," said Afron. "I understand well your father's sadness, for my horse of power, Chestnut-Grey, was taken by Tsar Berendey and I long for this great animal to be mine again."

"Allow me to clear my name by returning this horse to you," said Ivan.

"Very well. Do so and I will pardon you," said Afron. "Leave at once, and take the Firebird and her cage. They are yours now, but whether as a prince or as a common thief is up to you."

Ivan took the cage and climbed back over the wall. With shame, Ivan told Grey Wolf all that had happened.

"Young master, why could you not use your handkerchief to stop your hand from burning?" sighed the wolf. "I can help you, though, so climb on."

Ivan held onto Grey Wolf's thick fur and they galloped off again to the tsardom beyond, over mountains, across lakes, through forests and around cities. It seemed like no time at all before they were outside the high wall of Tsar Berendey's palace.

"Over the wall are Berendey's stables," said Grey Wolf. "There, you will find Chestnut-Grey, Tsar Afron's horse of power. Take the horse, but do not touch his bridle."

Grey Wolf allowed Ivan to climb on his back to get over the wall. He ran quickly to the stables and found the horse of power, which had a golden mane, silver hoofs and a bridle of priceless jewels.

"How will I control such a beast with no bridle?" thought Ivan. So he gently loosened the reins and took the horse and bridle together.

No sooner had he done so than every single bell in Tsar Berendey's palace rang out, for the bridle was joined to them by a thousand invisible threads. Hidden guards jumped upon Ivan and threw him before Tsar Berendey.

"You robbed me of my horse and the bridle," shouted the tsar, who could see Ivan was a prince. "Explain yourself."

"Forgive me, Sire, I stole Chestnut-Grey for Tsar Afron who pines for the horse of power that belongs to him."

"I understand Afron's misery, for my own daughter, the Princess of Inexhaustible Loveliness, was stolen many years ago," said Berendey sadly. But then he grew angry again. "Had you come to me with Afron's request I would have given you the horse, for it is indeed his. But the bridle is mine and therefore the crime is severe."

"Allow me to clear my name, Great Tsar," said Ivan. "I will recapture your beloved daughter and return her safely to you."

"Young Tsarevich, do this and you will be rewarded with her hand in marriage. Yet I fear it is impossible, for she is the prisoner of Kastchey-the-Deathless, the sorcerer of the dead. He is thousands of years old, for his death is hidden. No one knows where he keeps it and because of this he cannot die."

"Then I will find his death and defeat him in order to return your daughter to you," said Ivan.

"Take the horse of power and his bridle; they are yours," said Tsar Berendey. "But whether as a prince or a common thief is now up to you."

Ivan took the horse of power to where Grey Wolf and the

Firebird were waiting. Red-faced, Ivan related the whole story.

"Foolish Tsarevich," sighed Grey Wolf. "You should have used your belt to harness the horse. But do not worry, I can help you. Climb on my back and hold tight."

Ivan did what Grey Wolf told him, and holding the cage of the Firebird, and the bridle of Chestnut-Grey, they set off once more. Through the next tsardom and beyond Grey Wolf raced, and it was a good thing that Chestnut-Grey was a horse of power, or he would surely have been left behind.

At length it began to grow dark and it was soon darker than midnight. Fortunately, the Firebird lit the way, so Ivan soon saw that they had reached Kastchey's evil realm.

"You must go alone, young Tsarevich," said Grey Wolf sadly. "Take the princess, but leave her silver and golden slippers."

Inside a castle, in a tall tower, slept the Princess of Inexhaustible Loveliness. So lovely was she, that although the castle was hung with a thousand mirrors, none could show her beauty at once because there was so much of it.

Every day she searched for her captor's death.

"Perhaps my death is in the broom by the door," Kastchey would say. But when the princess broke the broom, she knew it was not there for the sorcerer did not die.

"Perhaps it is in an egg," he would say, so the princess had egg for breakfast. But still the old wizard lived.

"Perhaps it is in my daughter's tears," Kastchey said.

But Kastchevna, his daughter, had never shed a tear in all

her life, for though she was beautiful her heart was made of wood.

Ivan quickly climbed the vines that clung to the tower, slipped though a window and found the Princess of Inexhaustible Loveliness asleep on a great bed. She awoke at once, but when she saw Ivan she was not afraid, for he had a kind face.

She was indeed lovely and Ivan fell in love with her straight away.

"Quickly, your Loveliness," he whispered. "We must not delay." He carried her to the window and told her to hold on to him as he climbed back down the vine. But the princess was wearing her silver and golden slippers and all the alarms in Kastchey's castle rang out, for the slippers had been attached to them by a thousand invisible threads. Kastchey and Kastchevna ran outside and waited at the bottom of the tower.

"Thief!" squealed Kastchey, when Ivan and the Princess reached the ground. "How dare you take what is mine?"

But by the light of the Firebird's feather Kastchevna saw Ivan's handsome face and she felt a green shoot bursting out of her wooden heart.

"Father, do not harm the prince," she said.

Kastchey was most surprised, but he saw that his daughter had fallen in love with Ivan so he said, "If the prince will stay by his own choice, the princess can go free."

Ivan knew not what to say, for he loved the princess and wanted to free her, yet could not bear to be parted from her.

The princess herself spoke before he could. "Ivan cannot stay, for I love him and only death can part us!"

Kastchevna looked so disappointed that the Princess Loveliness was filled with pity for her. She stepped forward and kissed her on the forehead. Kastchevna's wooden heart split in two. She covered her face with her hands and wept, great tears splashing on the earth. Then roots shot out of her shoes, branches from her sleeves, until the tears fell not from Kastchevna but from the leaves of the weeping willow tree she had become.

"My death!" screamed Kastchey, for it really was hidden in his daughter's tears, and he crumbled like a dry leaf before their eyes. His cry was so loud it was heard by Tsar Berendey and Tsar Afron and Tsar Dadon, so many tsardoms away.

Ivan took the princess by the hand and together they pushed open the great rusty gates of Kastchey's realm and ran out into the sunshine beyond.

Then they climbed upon Grey Wolf, one holding the Firebird's cage, one holding the bridle of Chestnut-Grey. And they set off at such a pace that within a day they had arrived at Tsar Berendey's palace.

The tsar had never known such happiness. "Tsarevich, you have cleared your name with me. Chestnut-Grey and his bridle are yours as a prince, and my beloved daughter, Loveliness, shall be your bride tomorrow morning."

So the next day Ivan married the Princess of Inexhaustible Loveliness. As soon as the feasting was over the two of them climbed upon Grey Wolf and set off with Chestnut-Grey and the Firebird for the realm of Tsar Afron. Back across the forests and lakes they flew, past cities and over mountains, and by nightfall they had put Chestnut Grey back in Tsar Afron's stable.

"You have cleared your name, Tsarevich," said the delighted tsar. "Take the Firebird and her cage, they are yours as a prince!"

And so Ivan, the princess and the Firebird set off upon Grey Wolf once more, to the end of the tsardom and across the thrice-nine realms. All too soon, Grey Wolf came to the crossroads where he had eaten Ivan's horse.

"I leave you here, little master, for I have repaid my debt."

So Ivan embraced his friend and then he set off with his beautiful bride and the Firebird for the long walk to his father's palace. But along the road they encountered two noblemen on horseback. At first Ivan could not see who they were, but as he got closer he saw it was his own two brothers, Dmitri and Fyodor, returning from their unsuccessful quest.

"Ivan has captured the Firebird," hissed Dmitri.

"And he has taken a wife of breathtaking loveliness," growled Fyodor. They both boiled with jealousy and, as Ivan embraced them, they stuck their knives into his heart and carried off the princess and the Firebird.

For three days Ivan lay dead by the roadside, while his brothers were welcomed by Tsar Dadon as heroes. Dmitri took half his father's tsardom, Fyodor decided to take the princess for his wife. The princess had been struck dumb by the sight of her beloved's death and so could not tell the tsar the truth.

But on the night of the third day, Grey Wolf saw something glowing at the side of the road. It was the feather of the Firebird, still in Ivan's cap. Seeing the fate that had befallen his dearest friend, Grey Wolf lay down beside him and wept. All at once the sky was filled with a brilliant light. The Princess Loveliness could not speak herself, but she could free the Firebird and had done so. The Firebird flew to where Grey Wolf and Ivan lay. She took the feather from Ivan's cap and said:

"Weep not, Grey Wolf, this feather gives me the strength to serve our friend. I will fly to the ends of the earth to find the Water of Life, but I must hurry for Tsarevich Fyodor marries the Princess Loveliness in the morning."

With that, she flew off like a spark from a chimney across the black sky.

Whether it was a long time or not, who knows? For a deed takes time but this tale is nearly told. The Firebird reached the ends of the earth where a clear stream ran from a spring in the ground.

As she filled her beak, the stream said, "If I give you a life, you will owe me a life."

"Then I shall give you mine," said the Firebird, knowing she had found the Water of Life. Quickly she flew back to the other side of the world to where Grey Wolf had waited patiently. The Firebird sprinkled the Water of Life onto Ivan. This done she lay down upon the ground and died.

Ivan opened his eyes and said, "My goodness, how well I have slept!"

"But for the Firebird you would never have awoken," said Grey Wolf.

Ivan looked down at where the Firebird lay. She no longer burned; her feathers were cold and ashen.

"Who did this to you, my noble creature?" he cried.

Then he saw the feather was gone from his cap and he remembered the Firebird's promise to serve him with her life. Tenderly he lifted her off the ground and sobbed with grief.

"We must hurry, Prince," said Grey Wolf. "Your brother Fyodor weds your wife today."

Already the sun had risen in the sky. Ivan set off upon Grey Wolf with the Firebird held gently in his arms. They burst in upon the ceremony just as Fyodor was about to place a ring on the princess's finger. Her face was wet with tears, but the instant she saw her beloved Ivan her voice came back.

"Thieves! Villains!" she cried, pointing in turn to Dmitri and Fyodor, and she told the tsar the true story.

The tsar cast his two eldest sons onto the ground. "May you be known across the thrice-nine lands and beyond as common thieves!" he bellowed. "For you are no longer sons of mine!" And the two of them fled from Dadon's realm never to return.

That evening Ivan built a fire and placed the Firebird in the flames. When the last feather had burned there appeared in the ashes a golden egg. It split in half and out flew the Firebird, reborn, brighter and more beautiful than ever before!

The tsar was so grateful to her that he allowed her to come and go from his garden at will and to eat from his tree of golden apples whenever she wanted.

For each apple she ate, she left a pip, and from each pip grew another tree. They were ordinary, simple apple trees, but every autumn they bore fruit of gold!

JORINDA AND JORINDEL

by

THE BROTHERS GRIMM

retold by

EDGAR TAYLOR

As a piece of storytelling, this matchless little tale must be one of the most haunting and magical in Grimms' entire collection. The very opening paragraph (see how much is told in a short space) places a reader inescapably in enchanted country, in the eerie beautiful wood itself. With its swift pace and its clear sharp detail it is like the experience of a dream. Yet nothing in the words or the plot itself ever goes beyond the bounds of traditional fairy tale. Even the witch – the old fairy, rather – does not break the story's spell by an ugly end. She simply vanishes.

There was once an old castle that stood in the middle of a large thick wood, and in the castle lived an old fairy. All the day long she flew about in the form of an owl, or crept about the country like a cat; but at night she always became an old woman again. When any youth came within a hundred paces of her castle, he became like stone, and could not move a step till she came and set him free: but when any pretty maiden came within that distance, she was changed into a bird; and the fairy put her into a cage and hung her up in a chamber in the castle. There were seven hundred of these cages hanging in the castle, and all with beautiful birds in them.

Now there was once a maiden whose name was Jorinda: she was prettier than all the pretty girls that ever were seen; and a shepherd whose name was Jorindel was her sweetheart and they were soon to be married. One day they went to walk in the wood, that they might be alone, and Jorindel said, "We must take care that we don't go too near to the castle." It was a beautiful evening; the last rays of the setting sun shone bright through the high trees and touched the green underwood beneath while the turtledoves sang plaintively from the tall birches.

Jorinda sat down to gaze upon the sun; Jorindel sat by her side; and both felt sad, they knew not why; but it seemed as if they were to be parted from one another for ever. They had wandered far; and when they looked to see which way would lead to home, they found themselves at a loss to know what path to take.

The sun was setting fast, already half of its circle had disappeared behind the hill. Suddenly Jorindel looked behind him, and saw through the bushes that they had, without knowing it, come close under the old walls of the castle. He shrank for fear, turned pale, and trembled. Jorinda was singing,

> *"The ring-dove sang from the willow tree,*
> > *Sorrow! Sorrow! Sorrow!*
> *He mourned the fate*
> *Of his lovely mate,*
> > *Oh, sorrow, sorr— jugjugjug"*

The song ceased suddenly. Jorindel turned to see the reason, and beheld his Jorinda changed into a nightingale; uttering only a mournful *jug, jug*. An owl with fiery eyes flew three times round them, and three times screamed *Tu whu! Tu whu! Tu whu!* Jorindel could not move: he stood fixed as a stone, and could neither weep, nor speak, nor stir hand or foot. And now the sun went quite down; the gloomy night came; the owl flew into a bush; and a moment later the old fairy came forth, pale and meagre, with staring eyes, and a nose and chin that almost met one another.

She mumbled secret words, then seized the nightingale, and went away with it in her hand. Poor Jorindel saw that the nightingale was gone, but what could he do? He could not move from the spot where he stood. At last the fairy came back, and sang with a hoarse voice,

"Till the prisoner's fast,
And her doom is cast,
    There stay!
When the charm is around her,
And the spell has bound her,
Hie away! Away!"

And at that moment Jorindel found himself free. He fell on his knees before the fairy, and prayed her to give him back his dear Jorinda: but she said he should never see her again, and went her way.

He prayed, he wept, he sorrowed, but all in vain. "Alas!" he said. "What will become of me?"

He could not return to his own home, so he went to a strange village, and employed himself in keeping sheep. Many a time did he walk round and round as near to the hated castle as he dared go. At last he dreamed one night that he found a beautiful purple flower, and in the middle of it lay a costly pearl; and he dreamed that he plucked the flower, and went with it in his hand into the castle, and that everything he touched with it was freed from enchantment, and that there he found his dear Jorinda again.

In the morning when he awoke, he began to search over hill and dale for this pretty flower, and eight long days he sought for it in vain: but on the ninth day early in the morning he found the beautiful purple flower; and in the middle of it was a large dew drop as big as a costly pearl.

Then he plucked the flower, and set out and travelled day and night till he came again to the castle. Now he was less than a hundred paces away, and yet he did not turn into stone as before, but found that he could go close up to the door.

Jorindel was very glad to see this: he touched the door with the flower, and it sprang open. As he went within, he heard the voices of hundreds of singing birds. He followed the sound and came at last to a room where the fairy sat, with the seven hundred birds singing in the seven hundred cages. And when she saw Jorindel she was very angry, and screamed with rage; but she could not come within two yards of him; for the flower he held in his hand protected him. He looked around at the birds, but alas! there were many many nightingales, and how then should he find his Jorinda? While he was thinking what to do, he observed that the fairy had taken down one of the cages, and was making her escape through the door. He ran towards her, touched the cage with the flower, and his Jorinda stood before him. She threw her arms round his neck and looked as beautiful as ever, as beautiful as when they walked together in the wood.

Then he touched all the other birds with the flower, so that they again became young girls; and took his dear Jorinda home, where they lived happily together for many many years.

THE BOY WHO READ ALOUD

by
JOAN AIKEN

In Joan Aiken's world, old fairy tale and practical daily life, today or yesterday, live quite naturally together. There may be a clue here to her seemingly endless power of invention, whether in short tales or long novels. In the present story a tree can speak – but, more surprisingly – so can an old Rolls-Royce. (Aiken tales have a splendid disregard for time.) Choice of an Aiken tale was hard, as many will agree, but the item here seemed particularly fitting for this collection. And if the boy chances upon this book as he searches through libraries for yet more tales to read to his tireless listeners, he could come across his own story.

Once there was a boy called Seb who was unfortunate. His dear mother had died, his father had married again, and the new wife brought in three daughters of her own. Their names were Minna, Hanna and Morwenna, and they were all larger and older than Seb – big, fat, red-haired hateful girls. Minna pinched, Hanna tweaked hair and kicked shins, while Morwenna could pull such terrible faces that she put even the birds in a fright and her mother had forbidden her to do it indoors in case she cracked the cups and plates on the kitchen dresser. The mother was just as bad as her daughters, greedy, unkind and such a terrible cook that nine months after they were married Seb's father wasted away and died from the food she fed him on. As for Seb, he had to manage on crusts, for that was all he got.

Now Seb had three treasures which his true mother had left him when she died. These were a little silver mug, a little silver spoon, and a book of stories. The book of stories was what he prized most, for when she was alive his true mother had read them aloud to him every day and as soon as he grew old enough to learn his letters he read them back to her while she did the ironing or peeled the potatoes or rolled out the pastry. So, now, when he opened the book, it was as if his true mother were back with him, telling him a story, and for a little he could forget how things had changed with him.

You can guess how hard Seb tried to keep these treasures hidden from his step-sisters. But they were prying, peering, poking girls, and presently Minna came across the silver cup hidden under Seb's mattress.

"You mean little sniveller, keeping this pretty cup hidden away!" she cried. "I am the eldest, it should be mine, and I'll pinch and pinch you till you give it to me!"

"For shame, Seb!" said his step-mother when she heard him crying out at the pinches. "Give the cup to your sister at once!"

So poor little Seb had to give it up.

Then Hanna found the silver spoon hidden under Seb's pillow.

"Let me have it, let me have it, you little spalpeen!" she screeched, when he tried to keep it from her. "Or I'll drag out every hair in your head."

And her mother made Seb give her the little spoon.

Now Seb took particular pains to keep his precious book out of view, hiding it first in one place and then in another, between the bins of corn, under a sitting hen, inside a hollow tree, beneath a loose floorboard. But one evening Morwenna found it tucked up on a rafter, as they were going to bed. Quickly Seb snatched the book from her and darted off to his attic room where he shut himself in, pushing the bed against the door. Morwenna was after him in a flash – though, mind you, it was only pure spite that made her want the book for, big as she was, she could no more read than a gatepost can.

"You'd better give it to me, you little mizzler!" she bawled through the door. "Or I shall make such a fearsome face at you that you'll very likely die of fright."

Seb trembled in his shoes at this threat, but he knew that Morwenna could do nothing till morning, since she was not allowed to pull faces indoors.

Huddling in bed, clutching the book to him, he decided that the only thing for him to do was to run away. He would get up very early, climb out of the window, and slide down the roof.

But where should he go and how should he live?

For a long time, no plan came to him. But at last, remembering the book in his hands, he thought, "Well, there is one thing I can do. I can read. Perhaps somebody in the world would like me to read stories to them."

"In the village," he thought, "by the inn door, there is a board with cards stuck up on it, showing what work is to be had. I will go that way in the morning and see if anybody wants a reader."

So at last he went to sleep, holding the little book tight against his chest.

In the morning he woke and tiptoed out of the house long before anyone else was stirring. (Minna, Morwenna and Hanna were all lazy, heavy sleepers who never clambered from their beds till the sun was half across the sky.)

Seb went quietly through the garden and quietly down the village until he came to the notice-board. On it there were cards telling of jobs for gardeners, jobs for cooks, jobs for postmen, ploughmen and painters. Looking at them all he had begun to think there was nothing for him when up in the top corner he noticed a very old, dog-eared card with a bit torn off. It said:

ELDERLY BLIND RETIRED SEA

WOULD LIKE BOY TO READ

ALOUD DAILY

What a strange thing, thought Seb. Fancy reading aloud to the sea! Fancy the sea going blind at all!

But still, he supposed, thinking it over, the sea could get old like anybody else, old and blind and bored. Didn't the emperor Caligula have chats with the sea, and who takes the trouble nowadays to even pass the time of day with his neighbour, let alone have a conversation with the ocean?

There would be no harm, anyway, in going to find out whether the job had been taken already. Seb knew the way to the sea because when his true mother had been alive they had sometimes spent days at the shore. It was about twenty miles but he thought he could walk it in a couple of days. So he started at once.

Now, had Seb but known it, the truth of the matter was this: the card had been up on the board such a long time that it had been torn, and some of the words were missing. It should have read:

ELDERLY BLIND RETIRED SEA CAPTAIN

WOULD LIKE BOY TO READ NEWSPAPER

ALOUD DAILY. APPLY WITHIN

Nobody ever had applied for the job, and in the end the sea captain had grown tired of waiting and had gone off to another town.

But Seb knew nothing of all this, so he started off to walk to the sea, with his treasured book of stories in his pocket.

It was still very early and few folk were about.

As he walked along Seb began to worry in case he had forgotten how to read aloud, because it was now a long time since his true mother had died. "I had better practise a bit," he thought.

When he had gone about five miles and felt in need of a rest he came to a gate leading into a deserted barn-yard.

"I'll go in here," he thought, "and practise my reading. Because there's no doubt about it at all, it's going to seem very queer reading to the sea till I've grown accustomed to it."

There was an old rusty Rolls-Royce car in the yard, which looked as if it had not been driven since the days when ladies wore long trailing skirts and you could get four ounces of bull's-eyes for a halfpenny. Seb felt rather sorry for the poor thing, so broken-down, forlorn and battered did it seem, and he decided to read to it.

He sat down cross-legged in front of the radiator, took out his book and read a story about the sun-god's flaming chariot, and how once it was borrowed by a boy who had not passed his driving-test, and how he drove the chariot, horses and all, into the side of a hill.

All the time Seb was reading there came no sound or movement from the car. But when he had finished and stood up to go, he was astonished to hear a toot from behind him. He turned himself about fast, wondering if somebody had been hiding in the car all the time. But it was empty, sure enough.

Then he heard a voice, which said,

"Was that a true tale, boy?"

"As to that," said Seb, "I can't tell you."

"Well, true or not," said the voice (it came from the radiator and had a sort of purring rumble to it, like the sound of a very large cat), "true or not, it was the most interesting tale I have ever heard. In fact it was the *only* tale I have heard, and I am greatly obliged to you, boy, for reading it to me. No one else ever thought of doing such a thing. In return I will tell you something. In a well in the corner of the yard hangs a barrel of stolen money; five days ago I saw two thieves come here and lower it down. Wind the handle and you will be able to draw it up."

"Did you ever!" said Seb, and he went to the well in the corner and turned the handle which pulled the rope. Up came a barrel filled to the top with silver coins.

"There's too much here for me," Seb said. "I could never carry it all." So he took enough to fill one pocket (the book was in the other), wound the barrel down into the well again, and went on his way, waving goodbye to the Rolls-Royce car as long as he could see it.

He bought some bread with his money at the next village, and a bottle of milk.

After another five miles' walking he began to feel tired again, so he stepped aside from the road into the garden of an old empty house.

"This would be a good place to read another of my stories," he thought.

So he read aloud a tale of two friends who arranged to meet one night near a hole in a wall. But they were frightened away by a lion and so they missed seeing one another.

When Seb had finished he heard a harsh voice behind him (he was sitting with his back to the house) which said: "Was that a true tale, boy?"

"As to that," said Seb, "I can't tell you."

"True or not," said the voice, "it has given me something to think about in the long, empty days and nights. I never heard a tale before. So in return I will tell you something useful. Growing in my garden you will find a red flower which, if you pick and eat it, will cure any illness."

"But I haven't got any illness," Seb said. "I am quite well."

"If you eat this flower you will never fall ill, in the whole of your life. But take care not to pick the yellow flower which grows next to it, for that is poisonous and would kill you at once."

Seb wandered through the garden until he found the red and yellow flowers growing side by side.

"'Twould be a pity to pick the red one," he thought, "so pretty it looks growing there. Anyway I daresay somebody will come along who needs it more than I do."

So he thanked the house kindly and went on his way, waving until he was out of sight.

Presently it grew dark, so he ate some more of his bread, drank the milk, and went to sleep under an old thorn tree. Next morning, to thank the tree for watching over him all night, he read aloud a story about a girl who ran away from a suitor and turned herself into a laurel bush.

"Boy," said a rough, prickly voice when he had finished, "is that a true tale?"

"As to that," said Seb, "I don't know."

"True or not," said the voice, "I enjoyed it and it sounds true, so I will tell you something in return. Lodged in my topmost fork is the blue stone of eternal life, which a swallow dropped there a hundred years ago. If you care to climb up you may have it. Carry it in your pocket and you will live forever."

Seb thanked the tree and climbed up. The stone was very beautiful, dark blue, with gold marks on it and white lines. But, he said to himself, do I really want to live forever? Why should *I* do so out of all the people in the world?

So he put the stone back in the crotch of the tree. But, unknown to him, as he turned to climb down, he dislodged the stone again and it fell into his pocket.

He went on, waving goodbye to the tree as long as it was in sight, and now he came to the sea itself, with its green waves rolling up on to the sand, each one breaking with a roar.

"Will the sea be able to hear me if I read aloud?" Seb wondered.

Feeling rather foolish, because the sea was so very large and made so much noise, he sat down on the sand. Taking out his book he read first one story and then another. At first it seemed as if nobody heard him, but then he began to hear voices, many voices, saying,

"Hush! Hush!"

And looking up he noticed that all the waves had started to smooth out as if a giant palm had flattened them, so that hardly a ripple stirred as far as he could see. The water creamed and lapped at his feet, like a dog that wants to be patted, and as he waited, not knowing whether to go on or not, a long, thin white hand came out of the green water and turned over the page.

So Seb read another story and then another.

Meanwhile what had happened at home?

When they found Seb had run away the three sisters were very angry, but specially Morwenna.

"Just wait until I catch him!" she said. "I'll make such a face at him that his hair turns to knitting needles."

"Oh let him go," said the mother. "What use was he at all, but only a mouth to feed?"

None the less Morwenna and her sisters went off looking for Seb. They asked of this one and that one in the village, who had seen him, and learned that he had taken the road to the sea. So they followed after until they came to the barn-yard, and there they heard a plaintive voice wailing and sighing.

"Oh, won't some kind soul tell me a story?" it sighed. "Alack and mercy and curse it. I have such a terrible craving to hear another tale! Oh, won't somebody take pity on me?"

"Who's been telling you tales?" said Morwenna, seeing it was the old Rolls-Royce car that spoke. "Was it a little runt of a boy with a book he'd no right to sticking out of his breeches pocket? Speak the truth now, and I'll tell you another story."

"Yes, 'twas a boy," the old car said. "He read me from a wondrous book and in return I told him about the silver in the well."

"Silver in the well? Where?" screeched Minna and Hanna. Colliding together in their greed they made a rush for the well-head and wound up the handle. But Minna was so eager to get at the silver and keep her sisters from it that she jumped right on to the barrel when it came up, the rope broke, and down she went. So that was the end of Minna.

"Oh, well, never mind her," said Morwenna. "Come on, let you, for it's plain 'twas this way he went." And she hurried on, taking no notice at all of the poor old car crying out, "My story, my story!"

"Bother your story, you miserable old heap of tin!" she shouted back.

So they came to the empty house, and here again they heard a voice moaning and lamenting.

"Ochone, ochone, why did I ever listen to that boy's tale? Now I've nothing in me but an insatiable thirst to hear another."

"Was it a bit of a young boy with a little black book?" Morwenna said. "Answer me that and I'll tell you a story."

"Ah, it was, and in return for the tale he told me I showed him where to find the red flower that cures you of any sickness."

"Where is it? Where?" and the sisters went ramping through the garden till they found it. But in her haste to snatch it before her sister, Hanna grabbed the yellow flower as well, ate it, and dropped down dead on the very spot.

"Oh, well, she's done for," said Morwenna, and she hurried on, taking no notice of the old house which wailed, "My story, my story!" behind her.

"Plague take your story, you mouldy old heap of brick," she called back.

So she came to the thorn tree.

"Have you seen a boy?" she asked it. "Did he tell you a story?"

"Indeed he did, and in return I was telling him about the stone of eternal life in my topmost fork."

"Let me lay my hands on that same stone!" said Morwenna, and she made haste to scramble up the tree. But because she was such an awkward, clumsy girl she fell from the top fork in her greedy hurry, and hung head down among the thorns.

"If you'd waited a moment longer," said the tree, "I could have told you that the boy took the stone with him."

"Oh, you villainous old tree!" cried Morwenna, kicking and twisting, and making such faces as turned the birds pale in their tracks. But she was stuck fast, and hangs there to this day.

Meanwhile Seb's step-mother had married again, a man as mean-natured as she was herself. By and by they began to hear tales of a marvellous boy, who sat on the shore and read tales to the sea.

"And the sea's given him great gifts!" said one. "They say he's been shown where the lost treasure of the Spanish galleon lies, with cups of gold and plates of pearl and wineglasses all carved out of great rubies, and a hundred chests of silver ingots!"

"They say he's been told where every storm is, all over the world, and which way it's heading!" said another.

"They say he can listen to the voice of the sea as if it were an old friend talking to him!" said a third. "And devil a bit of a tide has there been since he began reading aloud, and a great inconvenience it is to the navigation in all the realms of the world!"

"Can that boy be Seb?" wondered the step-mother and her husband. They resolved to go and see for themselves. So they harnessed up the pony-cart and made their way to the sea.

Sure enough, there on the sand was Seb, reading away from his little book. So many times he'd been through it now, he and the sea just about knew it by heart, between them.

"Why, Seb!" says his step-mother, sugar-sweet. "We've been in such anxiety about you, child, wondering where you'd got to. Sure you'll be catching your mortal end of cold, sitting out on this great wet beach. Come home, come home, dear, for there's a grand cup of cocoa waiting for you, and a loaf with honey."

"That's very kind of you ma'am," Seb says back, all polite. "But if my sisters are there I'd just as lief not, if it's all the same to you."

"Oh, they've left," she says quickly. "So come along, dear, because the pony's beginning to fidget."

And without waiting for yea or nay she and her

husband hustled Seb into the pony-cart and drove quickly home. Didn't they give him a time, then, as soon as they got in, pinching, poking and slapping one minute, buttering him up with sweet talk the next, as they tried to find out his secrets.

"Where's the sunken Spanish galleon? Where's the plates of pearl and glasses of ruby and the hundred chests of silver ingots?"

"I'm not remembering," says Seb.

"Didn't the sea tell you?"

"Sure the sea told me one thing and another, but I was paying no heed to tales of ruby glasses and silver ingots. What do I care about silver ingots?"

"You little wretch!" she screamed. "You'd better remember, before I shake the eyes out of your head!"

"But I do remember one thing the sea told me," he says.

"What was that?"

He'd got his head turned, listening, towards the window, and he said, "The sea promised to come and help me if ever I was in trouble. And it's coming now."

Sure enough, the very next minute, every single wall of the house burst in, and the roof collapsed like an eggshell when you hit it with a spoon. There was enough sea in the garden to fill the whole Atlantic and have enough left over for the Pacific too. A great green wave lifted Seb on its shoulder and carried him out, through the garden and away, away, over the fields and hills, back to his new home among the conches and coral of the ocean bed.

As for the step-mother and her husband, they were never seen again.

But Seb is seen, it's said; sometimes at one great library, sometimes at another, you'll catch a glimpse of him, taking out longer and longer books to read aloud to his friend the sea. And so long as he keeps the blue stone in his pocket, so long he'll go on reading, and hearing wonderful secrets in return, and so long the tides will go on standing still while they listen.

Is this a true tale, you ask?

As to that, I can't tell . . .

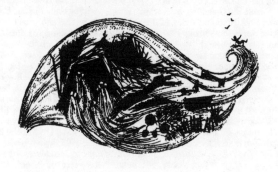

– ACKNOWLEDGEMENTS –

The publisher would like to thank the copyright holders for permission to reproduce the following copyright material:

Joan Aiken: The author and A.M. Heath & Co. Ltd. for "The Boy Who Read Aloud" from *A Small Pinch of Weather* by Joan Aiken, Jonathan Cape 1969. Copyright © Joan Aiken Enterprises Ltd. 1969. **Angela Carter:** "Little Red Riding Hood" from *Sleeping Beauty and Other Favourite Fairy Tales* chosen and translated by Angela Carter, Victor Gollancz 1982. This translation copyright © 1977 Angela Carter. Reproduced by permission of the Estate of Angela Carter c/o Rogers, Coleridge & White Ltd., 20 Powis Mews, London W11 1JN. **Stephen Corrin:** Faber and Faber Ltd. for "The Twelve Dancing Princesses" by the Brothers Grimm, translated by Stephen Corrin, from *The Faber Book of Favourite Fairy Tales* edited by Sara and Stephen Corrin, Faber and Faber Ltd. 1988. Copyright © Sara and Stephen Corrin 1988. **Vivian French:** "Tomkin and the Three Legged Stool" from *The Thistle Princess and Other Stories* copyright © 1995 by Vivian French. Reprinted by permission of Walker Books Ltd., London. **Naomi Lewis:** Reed Consumer Books Ltd. for "The Anklet" and "Friend So-and-So, Friend Such-and-Such" from *Stories from the Arabian Nights* retold by Naomi Lewis, Methuen Children's Books 1987. Copyright © Naomi Lewis 1987. Andersen Press Ltd. for "The Flying Trunk" from *The Flying Trunk and Other Stories from Andersen*, A New English Version by Naomi Lewis, Andersen Press 1986. Copyright © Naomi Lewis 1986. Penguin Books Ltd. for "The Goblin at the Grocer's" from *Hans Christian Andersen's Fairy Tales* translated by Naomi Lewis, Puffin Books 1981. Copyright © Naomi Lewis 1981. Naomi Lewis for "Hansel and Gretel" by the Brothers Grimm, retold by Naomi Lewis. Copyright © Naomi Lewis 1997. Nord-Süd Verlag AG for *Puss in Boots* by Charles Perrault, translated by Naomi Lewis, North-South Books 1990. Copyright © Nord-Süd Verlag AG, Gossau Zürich, Switzerland. Naomi Lewis for "Vasilissa, Baba Yaga, and the Little Doll" by Alexander Afanasiev, retold by Naomi Lewis, from *The Silent Playmate: A Collection of Doll Stories* edited and with an introduction by Naomi Lewis, Macmillan Publishing Co., Inc. 1981. Arrangement and original material copyright © Naomi Lewis 1979. A. & C. Black Ltd. for *The Wild Swans* by Hans Christian Andersen, English version by Naomi Lewis, Ernest Benn Ltd. 1984. Copyright © Naomi Lewis 1984. **James Mayhew:** David Higham Associates Ltd. for "The Firebird" from *Koshka's Tales: Stories from Russia* by James Mayhew, Kingfisher Books 1993. Copyright © James Mayhew 1993. **William Mayne:** David Higham Associates Ltd. for "The Tulip Bed" from *The Fairy Tales of London Town* Vol. I by William Mayne, Hodder Children's Books 1995. Copyright © William Mayne 1995. **Jean Morris:** Aitken & Stone Ltd. for "The Fairy God-daughter" from *Twist of Eight* by Jean Morris, Chatto & Windus 1981. Copyright © Jean Morris 1981. **Susan Price:** Faber and Faber Ltd. for "The Troll Bride" from *The Carpenter and Other Stories* retold by Susan Price, Faber and Faber Ltd 1981. Copyright © Susan Price 1981. Susan Price and A.M. Heath & Co. Ltd. for "The Princess and the Pea" by Hans Christian Andersen from *The Kingfisher Treasury of Nursery Stories* selected and retold by Susan Price, Kingfisher Books 1990. Copyright © Susan Price 1990. **Lore Segal:** "Rapunzel" from *The Juniper Tree and Other Tales from Grimm*, translated by Lore Segal. Translation copyright © 1973 by Lore Segal. Reprinted by permission of Farrar, Straus & Giroux, Inc. **Helen Waddell:** Mary M. Martin for "The Woman of the Sea" retold by Helen Waddell from *The Princess Splendour and Other Stories* by Helen Waddell, London 1969.

Every effort has been made to obtain permission to reproduce copyright material but there may be cases where we have been unable to trace a copyright holder. The publisher will be happy to correct any omissions in future printings.